MY HEART BELONGS TO A BOSS

A Mob Love Story

YASAUNI

Mz. Lady P Presents, LLC

My Heart Belongs To A Boss

Copyright © 2017 by Yasauni

Published by Mz. Lady P Presents

www.mzladypresents.com

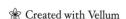 Created with Vellum

SYNOPSIS

Takhiya never had an easy life. Since the day she was thrown into this mean world, her fate had been decided. Living a life consisting of drugs and prostitution left Takhiya feeling like no one could help her, and she was alone in this jungle. All of that changes when she runs into LaQuan. LaQuan instantly sees past the life that she was thrown into and sees that she is crying out for help. He goes against everything he believes in to help a stranger, not knowing that this would change his life forever.

With a confirmation from the streets, LaQuan knows that he is as close to a king in the streets as he could get without actually being the king. He has everything that he needs to take over the west side of Chicago. He has a woman that supports him and a right-hand man by his side that would kill for him. Until he crosses paths with the wrong people and everyone he loves life is jeopardized, including Takhiya.

After having married the wrong woman, Bryce has promised himself never to love another woman. He runs into Takhiya and falls hard for her voluptuous curves and nonchalant attitude. Being the boss that he is, it's hard for him to hear the word no and not get what he wants. Being in a complicated position, Takhiya wants nothing to do with Bryce, but that's her problem and not his. Will she fight the inevitable or will Takhiya come to love his take charge demeanor and fall hard for a mob boss?

ACKNOWLEDGMENTS

First, I want to thank God because without him I don't know where I would be him. I would like to thank my mother Debra for listening to ideas I have. I have to give a big thank you to Trenae for helping me with this book and being there for me. Jaz' Akins you're the best and Mz. Lady P. for taking a chance with me. You're the best publisher a person can have. I have to thank my Auntie Bilhah for keeping her foot on my neck about me writing. When I told her I was taking a break, she might as well have told me break these nutz lol. To my cousin, Tiana and my friend, Kei thank y'all for bearing with me. I know I'm probably missing a lot of people but never charge it to my heart. I love all y'all and to my readers thank you!

Facebook: Yasauni Mc
    Instagram: Sauni
    Twitter: Yasauni McWilliams@sauniD

I dedicate this book to the McWilliams family I love all y'all ugly ass lol. We have our ups and downs, but no matter what, we rocking with each other. This book is especially dedicated to my cousin Rockhead live life to the fullest.

1

TAKHIYA

"Yes Bailey, I know, but I need to help Quan re-cop, so it's out of the question."

I could imagine the expression on her face as the sound of her smacking her lips came through my car speakers.

Bailey and I have been best friends since third grade; she was the new girl in the neighborhood. Our first day of school the school bully Patrice and her flunkies had Bailey cornered in the bathroom. I walked in just in time to see Bailey swinging her skinny arms trying to keep three girls off of her. I never liked any of the bitches anyway so I jumped in and helped her fight. We got our asses whipped together, got suspended together, and we've been like moths to flames ever since. Our rivalry didn't stop with Patrice that day though. We still to this day have beef with this bitch and have fought her on several occasions throughout college. People may think we're petty for it, but Patrice can't seem to mind her own damn business.

"Takhiya, fuck that nigga! He isn't shit and will never be shit. To this day, I don't know what you see in him, and I still wonder why you are fucking with his low life low budget ass. Who the hell sells drugs, but needs money from their girl to re-up? You've worked so hard to get where you're at now. The day you graduated from nursing school, he couldn't even buy you some flowers to congratulate you, but you sponsor everything he does. Bitch, you deserve this trip. Let's go celebrate. Having fun won't kill you, and trust me your grown ass child will be at home when you return."

As much as I love my friend, sometimes I just wanted to smack her in the mouth because she talked too damn much, but as usual, she was right. There was nothing that I wouldn't do for LaQuan. Even though for the last couple of years he has half stepped with me, LaQuan and I have a bond that goes back for years. I can honestly say I love him and no matter what, I will stand by him. It doesn't matter to me if he has money or not, I have my nigga back.

I guess you can say that coming from the environment I grew up in, I beat the odds. I am the daughter of dope fiend parents that sold me to every dealer that would buy me. At an early age, the dealers I was being sold to started giving me coke to numb the pain I felt and stop me from crying. As I got older, I learned there was nothing that I could control in my life but the drugs that were given to me in great quantity and food. So, I partook in the things that I could willing indulge in like coke and food.

By the time I was fifteen, I was a complete coke addict, and my afterschool activities were to turn tricks for my family's next fix. With the weight I put on, none of my parent's regular dealers wanted to touch me anymore, so we had no way to get what we needed. It took two days for my parents to get dope sick and start threatening me with bodily harm if I didn't find a way to get drugs for them. In their messed up minds, it was my fault that they were going through withdrawals, and not the fact that they directed themselves to this way of living. I realized I had been sober too long, and I was craving the coke high that I had grown love more than life itself.

I walked through my neighborhood for three hours before I ran into this guy I knew had exactly what I needed. Although I knew what he did, this was my first time actually having to ask the next nigga on the street for what I need. Once I built up the courage to approach him, I gave him a weak smile while standing in front of him.

"I will give you the best head you've ever had in your life for two blows and some raw."

He was a shocked, to say the least, and then began to look at me like he had never had head or pussy in his life. I began to feel uneasy by the way he was looking at me and turned to walk off. He eyeballed me up and down one last time before grabbing my sweaty hand and walking me through a gangway.

I squatted down in front of him as he pulled his dick out. The sight of his crusty ass penis made me want to throw up instantly, and if that wasn't bad enough, the smell was even worse. I jumped up backing away from him.

"What's the problem, you've never seen an uncircumcised dick before?"

"Nah, I'm good." I held my head down and turned to walk away from him. He reached out and grabbed me by my hair slamming me into the wall.

"You just wanted to give me the best head I've ever had, but since you don't want to give it willingly, I guess now I'll take it."

He held me up against the wall with one hand around my neck and began ripping the little clothes I had on off. Tears began to run down my face, but I didn't scream out. The truth is that I'm used to this kind of treatment, screaming never stopped the men before him, and I doubt it would stop him. I felt his grip get tighter around my neck, and I began to fade out a little when he screamed out at the top of his lungs.

I fell to the ground gasping for air, and I was now looking at the dark brown, tall, lanky guy with locs that hit his shoulders. His black eyes showed nothing but anger, and his nose was flared out as he sent blows at the guy until he fell to his knees.

"Greg, do you know rape will get you put under the jail and get you fucked in every hole you got, nigga?" The guy looked me up and down before he continued his assault on Greg. He kicked him hard in his side, Greg cried out in pain.

"Quan, you gonna stomp me out over a fucking coke head who asked for this shit?" Quan brought his Jordan's down in Greg's stomach. I looked at them sort of amused because Greg doubled Quan in weight, but Quan was about five inches or so taller than Greg. Greg laid on the ground not attempting to get up and defend himself.

"Naw nigga, I'm stomping you out over my fucking money you owe me." Quan's feet didn't stop moving until Greg somehow got into his pocket and started pulling knots of money out of his pocket and drugs with it.

My mouth started to water looking at the coke on the ground. I bent down to pick up the drugs I asked for, and Quan looked at me like he would beat my ass.

"Look ma; I've already stopped you from getting raped, now thank me and get the fuck on." I looked at him, and the tears started again.

"But, you don't understand. If I don't get the drugs for my parents they will do to me what you've done to him, but worse. I can't go home without these drugs; my dad will kill me."

My tears didn't move Quan; he looked at me and walked away. I dropped my head and walked out of the gangway crying like a baby. When I got back to the front, Quan was standing there.

"Yo, I ain't giving any drugs, but what I will do is buy you something to eat and take you to a shelter." I nodded my head yes and followed him to his car.

"Helloooo... earth to Takhiya!" Bailey screamed through her phone.

"What, bitch?" I snapped beginning to feel a little irritated with the entire conversation.

"I said my break is almost over. I'll hit you when I get off work." She didn't give me time to respond before my phone beeped to let me know she had hung up.

I pulled in my driveway blocking Quan's truck. I got out the car and grabbed the bags of groceries out of the passenger seat. I exhaled a breath glad I was able to get off work early. My plan was to cook my man dinner, cuddle, and fuck for the rest of the day. I walked into the front door and heard moaning, I left the door open so that I wouldn't disrupt whatever Quan had going on in my living room.

I continued to walk through the house with bags still in my hand until I saw Quan with a bitch bent over my couch banging the hell out of her.

"So, this is what you do while I'm busting my ass at work?"

LaQuan stopped mid-stroke, as the girl he was in couldn't control the shivering and shaking as she came on him.

"Baby, let me explain."

He pulled completely out of the girl and started walking towards me as his manhood slapped against his stomach. When he got in front of me stretching his arm towards me, I stepped out of his reach and looked past him at the girl as she was standing up facing me.

"Patrice." Her name faintly came from my mouth, as she stood there naked without an ounce of embarrassment with a smirk on her face.

You would have thought she had enough of me after the last fight we had because she was running her mouth about me. But no, she had to take it a step further and fuck my man in my house.

I dropped the bags down on the floor as tears came to my eyes, blurring my vision. I grabbed the object closet to me, which was the lamp, and threw it across the room grazing LaQuan's head.

"Nigga, this is how you do me after all these years? I take care of your stupid ass and break my back to make sure we cool, and you fuck the first thot you saw in the hood? Of all the hoes, you could've hit you chose this one?" I charged at him, punching him in his chest and face.

"Baby, she said she was going to call the police on me if I didn't fuck her. I can't go jail, so I did what was best for us!" LaQuan yelled out as he was trying to catch my hands to keep me from hitting him.

It went right over my head. I kept hitting him until I saw that bitch sitting on my couch naked as the day she was born, laughing like she had a bag of popcorn watching a comedy movie. I turned my attention to this smug ass bitch and charged at her. I jumped on the couch landing directly on Patrice lap knocking the couch backwards. I sent blows to her face as she tried to push me off of her, but my weight held her down. She gripped my hair and pulled my head down to her. She now had me at a disadvantage and flipped me over. She held onto my hair as she tried to hit me in my face, but I kept blocking her. She began to come closer to my face.

"Bitch, you can get a taste of what your nigga been eating for the last hour, I hope you enjoy it just as much as he did."

She started to move up closer to my mouth, and I bit her inner thigh as hard as I could. She started screaming and let my hair go. I pushed her off of me and blacked out punching her in her face I tasted the blood that was in my mouth and wasn't sure if it was mines or hers, but it made me angrier.

"You're going to kill her Khiya stop!"

LaQuan was yelling at me as he ran over to us and started pulling me off of Patrice. As he lifted me up, I made sure I got a good kick to her face. I snatched away from Quan, pushing him as hard as I could.

Quan helped Patrice off the floor. She looked a little dazed. Once she got steady, she looked at my hair in her hands.

"Nah bitch you got that ass whipped. You can't take these hands." She held my hair up and let the little bit she had swing.

"Bitch please; it's more where that came from unlike that beauty supply store shit you have in your head. By the time I get back downstairs you and this hoe better be out of my house."

I went to the room Quan and I shared and started packing my clothes in suitcases. I sat down on the bed because I was so furious my entire body was still shaking. I calmed myself down then continued to pack. When I walked back into the living room, Quan and Patrice were gone. My house looked a mess. I picked up the bags of groceries that were still by the door, turned out the lights, and walked out. I got in my car and found the song that I wanted and blasted it with tears in my eyes singing my heart out.

"It could all be so simple
But you'd rather make it hard...
Loving you is like battle
And we both end up with scars...
Tell me who I have to be...
To get some reciprocity
No one loves you more than me
And no one will ever will."

2

LAQUAN

When I met Takhiya, she was in a bad place in her life. With me being four years her senior, I never thought I would fall as hard as I did for someone so much younger than me. She was fifteen when I stopped Greg from raping her in the gangway. She was so caught up in trying to get the drugs she needed that she didn't care about me whipping that nigga ass in front of her. She tried to pick up the drugs that this nigga had promised her, but he owed me. She was more terrified of what her parents would do to her then she was of me.

That day I took her to get some McDonalds, questioned her about her parents, and dropped her off at a local shelter. Two days later, I found her sleep on my doorstep, and she still had on the outfit that I got her the day I dropped her off. We made an agreement, and my girl has been with me since then.

By the time she was seventeen years old, she had filled out real nice. She still had weight on her, but her five feet eight stature helped her carry it so well. Takhiya was all hips, ass, and breasts with a dark complexion. When she wore makeup, it perfected her beauty, and to top it off, she was a sweetheart with just the right amount of ratchet-ness. Her thick curly hair came to the middle of her back. She had a small gap in her teeth, dark brown eyes that were slanted and her skin is smooth and silky. I would say she reminds you of a black porcelain china doll.

Every now and then, she would walk around the house doing little flirty things, but I would ignore her. Right before her eighteenth birthday, I stumbled into the house drunk and bumped into her almost knocking her down. I reached out to grab her but ended up stumbling over my own feet taking both of us to the floor. We laid on the floor laughing for a second, and then Takhiya pulled my head down to her and kissed me.

"What you doing, ma?"

She rolled over getting my back to the floor and straddled me. "Taking what's mine." I decided then to let her have her way.

She unzipped my pants, and I started pulling her shirt and bra off. I pulled her down to me pushing her titties together sucking them. Takhiya started moaning softly. She kissed me again and began to move down on me. When she put my dick in her mouth, and I felt the back of her throat, I stopped breathing. Half the bitches I fucked with couldn't take me giving them the dick, and when they tried to suck it, they gagged on half of it.

She brought it back out of her mouth and sucked the head. She used her hand going up and down, but when she deep throat, she moved it. Her mouth was sloppy wet, and all I could do was hope her pussy was just as wet as her mouth. She had a way with my dick that every time she went down on it, I damn near jumped out my body. Takhiya was sucking my dick like she owned my shit. She pulled my dick out of her mouth, straddled me again, and slid down on my shit.

She started riding me, and at that point, I knew it was over. I felt like I had my own porn star. Her pussy was tight and so wet that I flipped her ass over on her back and gave her every inch of the dick. Once I got the last inch in, she squirted all over me. She tightened her pussy muscles on me, and I knew this shit was over. I increased my speed with every move I made.

"I'm coming, baby!" I pulled out of her, and she got up sucking my dick catching all my kids.

I could've resisted her, I could've sent her hot ass to her room, but

8

I had a soft spot shorty. I love Takhiya; she's the only woman that will ever have my heart. She has overcome so much shit just for me, to make me happy. My only problem is that my appetite for sex is greater than she can give me working and going to school full time. Hell, I'm a man, and I have needs.

I bought my truck to a complete stop and looked over at Patrice, she had a look of satisfaction on her face, and I couldn't understand why. Takhiya had beat one of her eyes close, her lips were split down the middle, and the side of her face was turning blue. My eyes roamed from her face to her body, and my dick began to stir in pants. Once the light changed green, I pulled off and kept my eyes on the road.

"Why are you sitting there so happy?" Patrice rolled the eye that wasn't swollen.

"Because I beat that fat stuck up bitch's ass." I cut my eyes at her and laughed.

"You beat her what?"

"Bitch please, can you even see out your right eye?" I blurted out before I realized.

I could tell she got mad at that question, but it is what it is, Takhiya tore into her ass.

"That's okay too because I got what I came for— you." She smiled at me and rubbed her hand down my left cheek as I spit the tea I had just drunk out.

"What? Patrice, you have lost your damn mind if you think I'm leaving my woman over a fuck that wasn't that good anyway. You and I are not a couple, item, or pair. It was just sex; you know how this shit goes."

Patrice's eyes went from happy to heated in a matter of seconds. I was barely able to react as punches came towards my face and head. I tried to block her as I swerved through traffic to pull the truck over. It was one thing for my girl to beat my ass, but it was another for some random rat to put her hands on me. I safely pulled the car over and backhanded her. She stopped swinging at me and touched her face.

"You're going to choose a fat coked out ass bitch over me. She could never give you what I can. She can't even be the type of woman that a real nigga like you needs on his arm. All her life she's been a low budget hoe, and that will never change."

I was passed the point of being pissed off, and I was angrier with myself than the hood rat in my passenger seat. She was right about two things though. Yes, I was choosing Takhiya over her, and she wasn't the type of woman that I needed on my arm. I have fallen off when it came to keeping Takhiya. I was being selfish as hell, and I have to find a way to make it up to her.

"Bitch, get out my car!" Patrice's eyes got big.

"But we are a thirty-minute drive from my house!" she yelled.

"You should have thought about that before you decided to insult my girl and my intelligence. Now get out before I drag you out, and we both know you don't want that." I stared her down letting her know not to play with me.

"I'm not going anywhere so do what you have to do." She sat with her arms folded across her chest.

I jumped out the truck mad as hell and ready to beat this bitch into a new personality and leave her on the curb. By the time I got to the passenger side of the truck, Patrice was hitting the gas so hard that she peeled off, burning rubber and leaving me in a cloud of smoke on the side of the road. I stood there appalled, cursing her out and pulling out my phone to call one of the fellas for a ride to the neighborhood. When I catch this bitch, I'm going to kill her.

3

PATRICE

I sped down the street and blew through the red light at the end of the block getting flashed by the red light camera. I knew once LaQuan got a hold of me he was going to beat my ass worse than Takhiya did, I don't give a fuck though. Any attention from him at all is good for me. I will take a couple of ass whippings if it keeps him happy. Most people would think I'm crazy; I'm not though. I just love that nigga no matter what he does and who he's fucking.

The bitch he has now isn't the bitch he needs by his side. I'm what he needs and what he will always need. If only he could see things the way that I see them. I don't know what he sees in that fat ass slob he calls wifey anyway. I mean she's average looking, has the average body, and an average ass job. She's a mediocre ass individual, and everything she has is because of Quan. Unlike me, I'm the prettiest bitch on this side of town, and I know how to be a down ass female for my nigga. I just can't understand what she has that I don't. He acts like this bitch leaks platinum when she comes.

People don't understand I have been in love with this man since I was twelve years old. I've been throwing pussy at him since I was fourteen, and he was ducking and dodging my shit like I had herpes or something. One day I walked up on him; I had to be about fifteen.

"Aye Quan, when are you going to stop acting like you scared of this pussy and come get it?" He looked at me laughing, and all his guys started laughing at me like it was a joke, but I was dead ass.

"Maybe if your lil' hood rat ass were older I would let you shake something for a real nigga. Didn't you know fifteen will get you twenty or life? I'm not trying to go to jail, and I hate to have to kill your daddy because you want to be a hoe. No thank you, ma! Now take your ass to school or go read a book or something."

Every one of them laughed at me, and I was livid. Who the fuck was he to talk to me like that? Instead of walking off like he said, I pulled my hand back to take a good swing at him, but he caught my hand before it touched his face.

"This is your first and only warning. If you ever put your hand up to hit me again, I will beat your ass, and then I will go beat your mama and daddy's ass for having a little bitch for a daughter." He pushed me down and stepped over me to walk off.

I sat there for a minute with my hands over my face. Everyone that was out that morning saw what happened to me, and I was passed embarrassed. I had made a fool of myself, and the neighborhood saw it. What pissed me off, even more, was the fact that Bailey and Takhiya's dirty ass was walking by. They laughed and stepped over me like I wasn't even there. If I wasn't feeling so self-conscience at the time, I would have tripped them.

The embarrassment was short lived and months pass by. My girls and I decided to go to the mall. Guess who I see walking out J-Bees with three bags in her hand and with who— Quan and Takhiya. I follow them through the mall and saw Quan footing the bill for everything she picked out. They even went in Footlocker to get matching Jordan's. I had to put an end to this shit. They walked out of Footlocker, and I blocked them from coming out.

"About two months ago I was too young for you, but this fucking crackhead is old enough? We have been in school together since kindergarten; she is the same age as I am. Her pussy may have more miles than mine, but that's the only thing she has on me." Takhiya put a little smile on her face and grabbed Quan's hand.

"I guess crackheads like myself know how to handle business better than a bitch that's been sucking dicks in alleys since she was ten."

"Says the bitch whose parents had her hoeing since she was two." Takhiya dropped Quan's hand and stepped towards me. Quan pulled her back to stand at his side, and Takhiya responded.

"That was by force now what's your excuse?" Quan laughed and pulled Takhiya to walk away.

"Fuck you Quan; you're no better than the bitch you're with so I guess that tells us more about the type of nigga you are— two crackheads in love. Takhiya, I guess you were striving to be like your parents, and when y'all have a kid, it will be the next you. Sold to the highest bidder and y'all have little crackish babies."

My girls and I laughed, but Quan turned around and looked at me crazy. Since I was on a roll, I threw my lemonade at him it splashed all over the front of him. He couldn't do shit to me we were in public. If he did try some shit, he was going straight to lock up. I felt real tough for making him look like a punk and embarrassing his ass the same way he did me. That was until he turned to Takhiya

"Beat her ass."

Takhiya's big ass ran into me like the linebacker that she was built like. When my back hit the floor, there wasn't a trace of a smile on my face. I tried to get up, but the blows she was sending to my little ass body was keeping me down. I looked at my friends, but Quan had them blocked from us. One of my friends attempted to run past him, but I saw him lift his shirt up to her. That was the last thing I saw before everything faded to black on me.

I hated the bitch even more as the years went on LaQuan kept her in the latest clothes and shoes. For her seventeenth birthday, he bought her a Lexus that she drove to school every day thinking she was shit. For her eighteenth birthday, he upgraded her to a Benz truck. To top all that shit off, this bitch wore a Gucci dress with a pair of thousand-dollar red bottom shoes on, and he rented her a Rolls Royce to come to prom in. I can't lie the bitch shut shit down with that, but all of that was supposed to be me.

I felt like he was flaunting this bitch in front of me to make me jealous because he knew my heart belonged to him. Even to this day, I love that nigga, and there is nothing I wouldn't do for him. My love has no limits whether it be bringing life into this world for him or ending that bitch's life he calls wifey. I rubbed my stomach and smiled. I stepped out of Quan's truck that I parked in front of his mom's house and dropped the keys before walking off.

❦ 4 ❦

BRYCE

I walked through Mariano's looking at what my brothers and I had accomplished. This has been a long three years of trying to get the family's business in order and grieving the deaths of our parents. To be honest, we were still in an ongoing war with some of the Italians, and trying to keep my brothers in order was the hardest thing to do. My brother Marcell was the worst of all us; he wanted to kill everyone. I had to stop him several times from walking in people's houses killing their families.

"Here are the papers you wanted." Jasmine walked up to me handing me the orders that I had asked her for. I smiled at her as she turned to walk away while making her ass jiggle.

"You might want to watch the way you're throwing all that ass around." Jasmine looked at me over her shoulder than bent over and twerked for me.

"There's nothing you can do with all of this." I began to walk towards her.

"I beg to differ, but we know you won't let me bend that ass over." I smacked her on the ass and watched it jiggle.

"Bryce, you know every time we even think about anything your brothers walk in and fuck up everything." I laughed at her. She was right, but my dick was about bust out my pants.

"You're scared of being watched, but fuck them. If one of them walks in, we will give them a show."

Jasmine was the manager of our club, but I fucked her from time to time. I swear her pussy would put a death grip on my dick every time I slide in her. I walked up behind her grabbing a hand full of her ass and pushing her over to the bar. When we got there, I pulled her dress up to her waist and grabbed her hair pushing her head down. I had just stuck my dick in her and was about three strokes in when my brother Marcell walked in the club. I started giving Jasmine deeper strokes, making her moan louder.

"This is not your office or a room, nigga." He started to walk back out the door but turned back around to me.

"Nigga you need to..." I pulled out of her right before my baby mama pushed Marcell out the way, I zipped my pants and walked from behind the bar getting ready for the drama.

"Who's this bitch, Bryce?" I laughed at her.

"Does it matter? You're more concerned about who I'm sticking my dick in then you are about the well-being of our child."

Olivia took off at top speed towards Jasmine who was standing there laughing at her. I grabbed Olivia around her waist and wondered what had I done so wrong to end up with this bitch as the mother of my child if I could call her that. Dogs took better care of their pups than this bitch did with our daughter.

"What the fuck you think you're doing? How about you run your ass to the house and see Justice for a change?"

"Fuck you and that bitch, Bryce." She turned and glared at Jasmine. "You better hope I don't catch you in these streets."

"It's fucked up you didn't hear shit I said about my daughter, but you want to fight some random bitch over me. Get your dumb ass out of my club."

I guess that made something click because she balled up here fist and started hitting me hard as hell. Marcell stood back laughing and watching the scene. It took everything in me not to hit her ass back. I picked her up off her feet and walked towards the door, Marcell opened the door, and I sat her ass on the other side. He closed the door when I stepped back in. It took both of our weight to keep it closed.

Olivia was a little ass woman. She was about four feet eight, maybe one hundred fifteen pounds, and strong as hell. We were finally able to lock the door, and Marcell looked at me laughing.

"The fuck you laughing at, nigga?" I bumped into him and kept walking.

"Nigga, why are you always letting her beat your ass and fuck up your day?"

I didn't want to talk to his goofy ass, so I went to my office. What really pissed me off more than anything is that I couldn't finish what I started because Jasmine had left. After an hour of bullshitting, I grabbed the keys and left with Marcell right behind me.

I walked to my Lambo and Olivia was standing next to it smoking a cigarette. I walked to the driver side, and she stood in front of me blowing smoke in my face.

"I saw your little bitch leave. You better be glad I'm in a good mood today, or I would have beat her ass too."

"Olivia my personal life hasn't been your business since you left me at the hospital with a crying newborn. Now get the fuck on." I pushed past her and got in my car. I reversed my car, and a fifth of Grey Goose bottle came crashing through my back windshield. Marcell looked at me and shook his head.

"What now bro?" I barely heard what he said because I wanted to run this bitch over.

I put my car in park, got out, and she flicked her cigarette in my face burning me a little bit. Before I knew it, I had smacked her ass to the ground.

"Bitch, you disrespectful. If you put this much energy into our child as you do into fucking up my life, we wouldn't have a problem in the world." I got back in my car.

"Bryce, I swear to God you gone pay for this shit. On my baby, you are."

"Bitch, if you had a baby, I would think you were serious, but since you don't, I ain't worried about it or you." I pulled off in my feelings about my window.

Olivia and I was the love story everyone wished for. Everything so happened fast with us. We met at one of my friend's parties and called ourselves falling in love at first sight. I remember it like it was yesterday. She had on some black jeans that fitted her ass just right. She had on a red loose fitting blouse that showed just a little of her stomach, and she had on a red Louboutin six-inch stiletto. She had on red lipstick that brought out her creamy flawless complexion and her blue eyes had me in a trance.

I wasn't even attracted to white women, but I felt her staring at me from the bar. I walked over to her, and her fiery attitude intrigued me. We sat at the bar talking for the rest of the night. We went out on a couple of dates, and by the third date, I was balls deep in her. Two and a half months later she went to my parents' house crying about being pregnant. My mother took one look at her and told me that I should have worn a condom. At twenty-two years old, I didn't want to hear what my mother had to say. I was in love, and my girl was having my baby. I would never turn my back on my blood, so I did the only thing a man like me would do, I married her.

I would say her pregnancy was the best part of our marriage. I became the attentive, loving husband that was soon to be a father. Seven months flew by, and before I knew it, we were at the hospital, and I was coaching her through pushing. She had the most beautiful baby girl, and our child had taken the best qualities from each of us. I was so happy, and I couldn't wait to show her off to the world and have family outings. I was going to be everything my dad was to his four boys and more to my daughter.

After the nurses cleaned my baby girl up and laid her on her mother to feed her, I looked at my two girls, and they were perfect in every way.

"So, what are we going to name?" Olivia frowned as she tried to give the baby her nipple.

"What are you thinking? I really hadn't picked out names for girls." Olivia continued to frown down at the baby.

"Since she's the spitting image of her mother what about naming her after you?" She turned her nose up as she moved the baby to the other side to take her breasts.

"God no Bryce, I hate my name. Did you know that a group back in the day made a song about a girl with my name that was a prostitute? I will not have my child going through that."

I laughed because I knew exactly what song she was referring to. The baby began to get fussy, so I reached to get her, and Oliva practically pushed her into my arms.

"What's wrong, babe?" Oliva's eyes began to tear up as the baby calmed down in my arms sucking her fingers.

"She won't even take my milk. Bryce, I feel like I'm defected or something, and she knows it." Oliva pointed at the baby, our baby, and looked at her like she was a foreign species in my arms.

"Babe, you're not defected, trust me I know. We will get her a bottle for now, and you can try again later. I'm pretty sure things like this happens to a lot of moms." I looked at the nurse who was in the room, and she nodded her head yes.

"See babe, don't worry about it. With some time and patience, she will be drinking your sweet nectar soon. Oliva rolled her eyes at me but smiled a little as she watched me feed the baby.

"How about Jessica? I think she looks like a Jessica." Oliva laughed.

"Gosh no! We'll think of something before we leave, ok."

I nodded my head in agreement and continued to feed my beautiful baby girl. She had me thinking about leaving the business, and I really wasn't into yet, but I didn't want to jeopardize my freedom or life when I had my child and wife to look after. Throughout the night, the baby was crying to be feed and Olivia would try to give her nipple, but the baby just wouldn't latch on. I continued to encourage Olivia that she would eventually get the concept. I then would stay up and feed the baby.

I woke up around six that morning to my baby was screaming at the top of her lungs and an empty room. I realized where I was and gazed around the room figuring Olivia had gone to the bathroom. I picked the baby and gave her a bottle, burped her, and rocked her back to sleep. Olivia still hadn't come from the bathroom, so I walked over and opened the door no one was there. I looked at the chair that her bag was in and it was gone, but there was a letter sitting there.

My dearest Bryce,

When I first laid eyes on you, I envisioned our future. I saw you as my loving husband and me being your doting wife and a loving mother. I envisioned the perfect four-bedroom house with a white picket fence. We would have three kids two boys and a girl that would have looked just like me but have your dreamy brown eyes. We would have spoiled all our kids rotten, but my daughter would have been the apple of my eye and would have you wrapped around her little fingers. As I sit here writing this letter to you my heart aches knowing that I have birthed a child into this world, and I can't even connect to her the way I should and the way that I want to. I've read that giving birth to a child is an emotional experience and once you lay your eyes on the little person that you have lived, eaten, and breathed for, for nine months that you instantly bond. The connection should be so powerful that you would want to die just so your child lives. Thank you for being so patient with me throughout this pregnancy, for caring for me, for being a loving husband. For that, I will love you with every beat of my heart. If it were just you and I in the world together, everything would be perfect, but after having this baby I know I'm not cut out for motherhood.

Olivia

I read the letter three times, and my heart broke each time I read it. The nurse walked in the room, and I was in a daze cradling my baby girl to my chest. I was trying to figure out how can a woman that I loved with my soul turn out to be so cold to leave her husband and child.

"Mr. Marino where's your wife?" I held the baby to me bringing her up to kiss her cheek.

"I'm trying to figure that out right now. When was the last time you saw her?"

"She asked me to step out so she can shower and dress about an hour ago." I knew then that I wouldn't find her until she wanted to be found.

I planned to take her home after the baby was born and show her how I had put everything together for her and the baby. I just knew it would make her the happiest woman on earth since I bought her the house she had been looking at for months.

She never made it there, Justice and I went home by ourselves to a big ass house and no one to share it with. My baby didn't even have a name when we got home, after days of sulking and taking care of my baby. I looked at her pretty face, curly black hair and eyes that matched the sadness I had in mine and named her Justice. I knew that when her mother got what she had coming to her that shit would be served cold. The day she left me left a bad taste in my mouth for women. Don't get me wrong I do me every chance I get, but I will never let a woman get close enough to me to break me down like that.

I leaned back and glanced at the back seat full of glass and shook my head; I had to get this bitch off my mind. I had a little over a week to pull our grand opening off, but first I have to get my baby fixed and detailed.

5

BAILEY

"Welcome to Miami my name is John, and I'll be your driver for the day," the guy that held a sign with Takhiya and my name on it stated.

"Thank you, but I think you have the wrong people." I eyed him suspiciously.

He gave me a huge smile showing perfect white teeth.

"No, I'm sure that you two are one of a kind and can never be mistaken for anyone." He opened the door to the limo and stood back.

"That was real smooth John." I smiled at him as I stepped to get into the limo, and Takhiya snatched me by my arm pulling me out of the car.

"Khiya, what the hell is wrong with you?" she looked over at John.

"Excuse us, please." John nodded his head before Khiya turned her attention back to me.

"We didn't rent this so why are you getting in it? Bitch, people are coming up missing every day and you jumping on the first nigga in Miami that knows our name." She stood there with a serious expression on her face waiting for me to respond.

"First off, no one in this world wants two ghetto bitches from

Chicago. We would be more of a problem to them than a solution to whatever they have going on. Can we be great for a change?"

I walked back over to the limo and got in. I saw a card across from me. I picked it up looking in it, and handed it to Takhiya.

"It's for you."

She grabbed the card reading it aloud.

"I will make this up to you, don't leave me. LaQuan?" She stood with her mouth open.

"I told you that nigga wasn't broke. I almost feel bad about what I did to his car now." I couldn't help but laugh.

"Get in, Khiya."

One day ago

I walked in the house tired as hell from work, of all the things to be life why would I choose a Cosmetic Chemist. Oh yeah, I forgot I wanted to make ugly bitches look pretty. I closed the door behind me and hung my purse up on the hook by the door. I kicked off my shoes and walked into the dark living room turning on the light. I jumped back with my hand on my chest as my heart pounded against my rib cage.

"Takhiya, why the fuck are you sitting in here in the dark? You damn near gave me a heart attack." I walked past her going to the bathroom. I came out talking a mile a minute going to the kitchen and looking in the refrigerator.

"Are you planning on cooking something I know there was nothing in here when I left this morning?"

I turned to her, and for the first time since seeing her in there, she looked so defeated and broken. I walked over to the couch and sat down seeing the swelling in her face that was starting to bruise. I quickly gave her hug and pushed her hair out of her face. I put my feet on my ottoman and got ready for the bullshit.

"What did he do?" I grunted.

I sat on the couch fuming as she painted me a vivid picture of what took place at her house this afternoon.

"You mean to tell me out of all the hoes in Chicago he chose the bitch that you hate most and have community pussy. I know this bitch has all types STD's ABC's and UFO's." Takhiya rolled her eyes at me.

"You are not making me feel any better about this." She looked down at her hands and began fidgeting with her fingers.

"Khiya, what did you expect out of this nigga? He's been cheating on you on and off for the last couple of years. Just because this nigga tells you he had an epiphany, you take him back every time. You need to leave his trifling ass and find you a new worthier man and not a little boy." Takhiya gave me the saddest look I've ever seen in my life.

"You don't understand Bai, LaQuan has saved my life more than once. He stopped Greg from raping me all those years ago in the alley, but what you don't know is that once he stopped Greg, he dropped me off at a shelter." I let my mind drift back to the reason I would never leave LaQuan.

It was my second day in the shelter, they had turned the lights out, and I laid on the cot that was assigned to me. I tucked the rest of my belongings that weren't stolen the night before under my head and body once I laid down. I tried to get comfortable on the piece of cloth connected to steel poles, but it wasn't working out too well for me. Suddenly I was snatched down to the floor, and someone covered my mouth.

I tried to scream out as the dirty face of a man came to face to face with me. He pulled at my jogging pants, forcing his fingers in me and smiling.

"Yeah, this is going to be good." He brought his hand up to face and smelled my scent on his fingers.

I couldn't move because he put all his weight on top of me. As he tried to adjust himself and me to enter me, he moved his hand from my mouth a little. That gave me the movement I needed, and I bit the hell out of his hand. He screamed out in pain and moving off of me, and I jumped up getting my bag off the cot. I looked around the room, and everyone on that side of the room was looking at me. I ran out of the door and walked half the night. I ran into Greg; he had a cast on his arm and was walking with a limp.

"I need Quan's address." He looked me up and down.

"What are you going to give me for it?" I looked him in the eyes.

"How about I not tell Quan that you were trying fuck with me again?" Greg laughed.

"Bitch please, you're just some random hoe that he just so happened to save. If he wanted you to have his address, he would've given it to you now bye Shelia."

Now that shit pissed me off, and I was tired of being the victim, so I kicked him in his fucked up leg. He dropped to one knee, and I kicked him in his hip.

"Okay, he stays at the end of this block the brown house on the corner with the black gate." I kicked him again

"And it's bye Felicia, bitch."

I walked to his house. It was too late to knock on his door, so I sat on the steps put my bag under my head and fell asleep. I woke up the next morning being shaken.

"Please don't hurt me." I balled up on the steps and didn't look up to see who was trying to get me up.

"Aye ma, what are you doing at my house? How the hell did you find out where I stay? I know you hear me talking to you."

I sat up and looked at LaQuan. His dreads were freshly twisted into a different style from when I last saw him. He had on a crisp white t-shirt some Levi 501 and a different pair of Jordan's from when he stomped Greg out. He stood over me staring at me, and he was furious.

"I guess you can't talk now, huh? If you're here for drugs, ain't shit shaking. Now get the fuck off my porch before I throw your chunky ass over the gate."

I stood up with tears in my eyes, as he looked at me disgusted. I was going to walk away, but I just looked at him and broke down.

"I've told you before tears don't move me." I turned to him.

"I'm sorry I came here thinking you would help me. I'm just so tired of all the bullshit. I fucking hate that my dad's nut connected with my mom's egg. My life has been fucked up ever since I came into this world. Everything and everyone that I have tried to get help from has always turned their back on me or wanted to fuck me in exchange for help. I know you dropped me off at the shelter, and I appreciate that you even considered doing it, but I couldn't even sleep in that place. The first night I was there someone stole the clothes you had bought me and last night some old ass white guy tried to rape me. I'm just so tired. I'm tired of selling pussy, I'm tired of the drugs, and I'm tired of this fucking life." I walked down the stairs and turned to him.

"Thank you for making me realize that my life isn't worth living." I walked out the gate and was getting ready to walk into the morning rush hour traffic.

"Takhiya, come here." I walked back over to him tears still rolling down my face and snot coming from my nose.

"What?" He gave me a look letting me know he wasn't up for the attitude, but I didn't care. I was a half a second from killing myself.

"What Quan?" He nodded his head

"How old are you?" I looked down at the shoes he had gotten me from Walmart.

"I'm fifteen." He paced his front porch for a minute.

"And where do your parents stay?"

"1540 North Rockwell." He walked down the stairs and looked at me.

"I'm going to help you; you can stay with me. You know the lifestyle I lead and what I do to get my money. I can't have a crackhead staying with me, the only way this will work is if you really want to quit. Takhiya if I find out any of my merchandise or money is missing out of this house. Suicide will not be an option for you. You get me and don't think it will be an easy death."

He stared at me in a way that I knew he wasn't playing, but he was doing something no one had ever done for me, which was giving me a chance. He went and unlocked the door to the house

"Go sit down until I get back."

I looked over at Bailey after telling her what happened and I could tell she didn't give not one fuck about the past.

"Takhiya, ok he saved you, but what about all this shit he is doing to you now. You can't possibly think it's ok for him to treat you this way. Takhiya looked at me like she was drained and confused.

"What do you want me to say? I'm your friend, and my job is to keep it real with you." Takhiya looked at me as I got off the couch and started pacing the floor I was heated. This nigga has played my girl for the last time, and this bitch Patrice will think twice before she decides to put that black hole she calls a pussy on anyone else's man.

"Bai, I just need you to be here for me," she finally let out.

I nodded my head at her and walked into my room stripping out of my work clothes. I put on a black jogging suit and some black Air Max. I walked back into the living room with a bat in my hand. I looked at Takhiya sitting there looking like a sad puppy.

"Get dressed." Takhiya looked at me weird.

"Why? What are you going to do?" I smiled at her.

"I'm going to be there for you now come on," I replied while grabbing another bat out of my hall closet handing it to her.

Takhiya and I went to the hood when we pulled up on Patrice I saw there was no need to put hands on her, Takhiya had fucked her up pretty bad. Just as I was telling Khiya that we were just going to leave her alone, this bitch had to open her open her mouth.

"I see you came out to get that ass beat a second time today." Patrice tried to put on her tough front in the presence of her friends. They all laughed at her statement, and Khiya and I jumped out the car swinging bats at them hoes.

We beat their asses. What most people forget is that Takhiya and I are just as hood as they are. We just chose to have careers instead of thoting the streets like most of the females we went to school with.

That nigga Quan couldn't be found at all, but when I saw his truck outside of his mother's house, we put in work on it. Most simple-minded females would have keyed the car and busting his windows, but not me. I let the air out of his front driver tire and the back tire of the passenger side so when he pulls off his car would wobble down the street. I picked up the keys that were on the ground next to the car, I opened the doors and cut his seat belts, and then I popped the hood took all his spark plugs and unscrewed pieces to the engine. I hope when he comes back he gets in the car, closes the door and his engine drops to the ground.

As we rode in the back of the limo, Takhiya looked at me.

"Bailey, I have been with this man since I was seventeen, what am I going to do without him?"

I know her love runs deep for this nigga, but she wasn't going to start all this and mess up our vacation. I took my shades off before speaking.

"The first thing that will happen is you will enjoy yourself. Secondly, when we get home, you will notice how much money you will save without his sorry ass being around, and third, you will find a man that will dick you down and take your mind off of his low, bottom of the borrow, maggot, sorry excuse of a man. You better not let one tear drop out of eyes because right now LaQuan is a non-motherfucking factor, you got that?" She seemed to cheer up a little, and that's all that mattered.

"You're the best, Bailey," she chimed I smiled at her before replying.

"Tell me something I don't know."

6

TAKHIYA

"You ready to go to the pool?" Bailey walked in my room that was connected to hers in her white two-piece bathing suit ready to go to the pool.

We had only been here about thirty minutes, and Bailey was ready to go out and party, but I wasn't; my emotions were all over the place. I had some hard decisions to make. I can't live my life like this. Every time LaQuan did some shit this dumb, it always made miss the high that made me feel so free and in control of myself and emotions. I looked my friend over, and she looked cute in the pieces of cloth she had on.

"Go ahead Bailey; I'm going to stay in the room today." I walked over to my bags and started pulling clothes out to take a shower. I felt Bailey's eyes on me the entire time.

"I know you're not letting that nigga take up space in your head. You're here so you won't have to think about him and the bullshit he's put you through." I sat on the bed.

"I'm just not feeling it today. Just give me this one day, please." Bailey raised her eyebrow at me and put one hand on her hip.

"Ok you can have today, but tomorrow you're going to act like you've never met LaQuan. If you're lucky, you will find a man that can take your mind off of him, and if I pray real hard, maybe we can get you drunk fly you to Vegas and make the nigga marry you." Bailey turned and walked out the door, and I laughed walking to the shower.

I got out the shower put on my favorite perfume and lotion and put on some little shorts and a tank top to chill in. I walked over to the bar in the room and pulled the Hennessy and a glass. I poured myself a glass sat and gulped it enjoying the burn as the liquor went down. I picked the bottle up, poured another cup, and reflected on the shit I had been through with LaQuan and all I could think was is he worth it.

A couple of hours had gone by, and Bailey wasn't back yet, so I decided to go down to the pool to make sure she was alright. I stepped on the elevator, and my heart stopped beating. The man that stood there was the finest I've ever seen in life. I mean I could go around the world die and come back, and he would still be the finest man I've seen in my life. His presence demanded attention and respect; it was like he consumed the entire space.

He was dressed in all black slacks, a dress shirt, and vest. I could tell from his extremely light complexion and jet-black hair that laid to his head that he was mixed. I looked down at his shoes and could tell that they were expensive leather. He was about six inches taller than I was, and I could tell from the tailor-made clothes he had on that he was built nicely. This man looked like old money, but he had a dangerous air about him. He let his eyes travel over my body, and I became self-conscience pulling at the shorts I had on like it would make them longer than they were. He kept his eyes on me than leaned back on the wall to get another look at my ass.

"Mmm... you smell good enough to eat." My skin felt warm, and if I weren't so dark, he would be able to see that I was blushing. I just smiled at him like an idiot.

"I've always had a thing for chocolate, especially dark chocolate." He licked his lips and winked at me.

"I'm not sure if I should say thanks for the compliment or run fast as hell out of here when the door opens again." He laughed at the statement.

"I'm harmless, I swear. I can tell you're not from around here."

"Is it that obvious? What gave it away, the fact that I'm not a size two?" He laughed.

"No, actually it was your accent. Where are you from?"

"Chicago," I replied quickly. He looked me over once more before the elevator doors opened, and we both stepped into the lobby.

"I have to get out of here now, but my name is Bryce what's yours."

"I'm Takhiya; it's nice to meet you." I held my hand out to him. He smiled and bent down kissing my hand while handing me a card.

"I usually don't pick up random women in the elevator, but I want to see you again. My cell phone number is on there text me. Let me take you out and show you around town."

I took the card smiled and walked away. I didn't have any plans on texting him. Hell, I'm not trying to a static and never make it home. I walked over to the trash to throw the card away but thought twice of it. I decided just to go to the pool and check on Bailey.

I got to the pool area and it was lit, the music was blasting if people weren't dancing they were drinking. I got to the middle of the area, and there was a lady on top of the table swinging her bikini top in her hand. She threw the top at my feet and blew me a kiss. I continued to walk around until I spotted Bailey at the bar on the opposite side pool. I came up behind her while she was talking to a guy that looked like the typical dope boy. As I approached them, I noticed how handsome he was and his green eyes looked as he was looking through me. Bailey turned around and looked at me before I could sneak close to her.

"You finally decide to drag your ass out of bed, huh?" I stepped to her side.

"Only because I ran out of Hennessy." Bailey got the bartender's attention and ordered me a drink. When he came back, he winked at me.

"This one is on the house." I smiled at him.

"Thank you!" He nodded and walked away. I turned my attention back to Bailey.

"Damn, I'm so rude. Takhiya, this is my new friend Marcus, and Marcus this Takhiya." Marcus smiled at me.

"I'm starting to think everyone in Miami is mixed and fine as hell, including the females," I told Bailey.

I'm not into women, but these bitches here are bad with pretty faces and nice ass bodies. It doesn't look as if they paid for them neither. I'm not the jealous type, and I don't mind giving females compliments.

"I think you're right. I haven't seen one ugly person yet. Damn, I spoke too soon." Bailey pointed to the corner where this lady was sitting with her eyebrows drawn on up to her hairline, and her makeup was three shades lighter than the skin that showed from her swimsuit. All three of us laughed.

We continued to talk and enjoy each other's company for the next hour until Marcus decided it was time to go. Before he walked away, he turned to me.

"Takhiya, I know I just met you, but from your persona and attitude, I know you and my bro would make a perfect match. How about we all get together the night before our grand opening and just go out." I looked at Marcus cautiously.

"I'll think about it." Marcus nodded his head and walked off. Bailey stood in directly in front of me giving me evil eyes.

"Damn Khiya, you're shooting him down like that."

"What did I do?" I was really perplexed about her attitude.

"He asked you to go out with us and meet his brother, and you acted like he asked you to share a bowl of soup with an Ebola patient."

"I just don't want to meet anyone and give them a sense of false hope of anything."

"He didn't ask you to fuck his brother on top of the bar either. Khiya, this is your one week to act like you're not committed to an asshole that can drop herpes in your lap the next time he sticks his dick in you. Damn live a little, have fun, find a dude, and fuck him every day that we are here. Act like that nigga Quan has dogged you out, so when you go home, you have finally have something to hide. This nigga Quan has your ass so trained you're faithful to the thought of him being faithful to you. Let that nigga fuck the world this week, and you won't care because you would have one up on him." I stood there as Bailey walked away leaving me at the bar nursing my second glass Hennessy; she always made valid points.

I finished my glass and went back to my room. I walked in and noticed I still had the business card that fine ass Bryce gave me. I sat it on the nightstand but knew I wasn't going to use it I turned the lights out and went to sleep.

⚬✵⚬

I WOKE THE NEXT DAY TO BAILEY LYING NEXT TO ME.

"Bitch, get up and get dressed. We're going to the mall." I rolled over to her.

"Damn Bailey, it's like eight o'clock in the morning."

"No, it's one o' clock in the afternoon; now get your drunk ass up."

I drug myself out of bed walking to my suitcase pulling out jogging pants and a t-shirt.

"Are you serious, Khiya? Just get in the shower; I got this."

I rolled my eyes at Bailey walking to the bathroom turning on the shower. I grabbed my Japanese Cherry blossom shower gel, lathered up, and started singing "Happy" by Mary J. Blige. I got out the shower combed my thick hair and braided it into a halo braid. When I came out, and Bailey had laid out my thigh length, white sundress and my all white flat Gucci sandals. I got dressed, put on a little makeup, and walked out the room.

"You look a lot better. I hope you're ready to have some fun because I didn't bring you here to feel sorry for yourself." She glanced up from her phone to look at me as we walked through the mall.

"I feel better, and I'm ready to enjoy myself."

I followed Bailey to the food court. My stomach started talking to me, and I walked off to grab a burger and fries. I found a clean table and sat down while Bailey was standing in the middle of the looking around. Marcus walked over to her, and they talked as I ate my food. I picked up some fries to put in my mouth but stopped because I felt like I was being watched. I checked my surroundings and didn't see anything out of place or anyone I know. I continued to eat my food when I saw someone's shadow standing over me.

"I love a woman with a nice appetite; it's refreshing to see a woman eat real food. Most women would have gotten a salad." I looked into the same eyes that stared me down on the elevator.

"I'm not most women." Bryce cut me off.

"I can see there's no comparison." He looked at me like he wanted to eat me alive. He sat down in front of me.

"I guess I'm not your type." I raised my eyebrow at him.

"Why would you think that?"

"Because I never got a call or a text from you yesterday."

"I was busy," I lied smoothly.

"Yeah, she was busy taking down her new man Hennessy." Bailey and Marcus walked over to us sitting down. Marcus looked at Bryce and me.

"Y'all know each other?" Bryce smiled.

"We met yesterday at the hotel, but I have a feeling Takhiya isn't feeling me like that." Bryce gave me a look that made me want to fuck him on top of the table in the middle of the mall. I swear this man was eye fucking me, and I felt every stroke of it. I crossed my legs squeezing them together to calm the pulsating that pussy my doing. Bryce looked at me and licked his lips, and I swear I came right then and there. I got up.

"I need to use the bathroom." I didn't understand what was going on; it's like this nigga had a personal connection to my pussy.

"Takhiya, wait up!" Bryce yelled out.

I continued to walk away from him. I didn't even know where I was going.

"I see you liked to be chased, I can handle that, but the bathroom is in the other direction." I stopped and turned around bumping right into him. My entire body flushed. Bryce pushed me against the wall, and my nerves were on edge.

"Look ma; I can tell from your reaction to me that if nothing else you want me to knock the bottom out that pussy. Like I said I'm up for the chase, but since you only have some many days here, we really don't have much time to play around. I'm not going to act like all of this is on you because I would love nothing more than to feel your pussy around this dick. If it were up to me, I would bend your ass over against this wall, but it's not. I know we just met, but it doesn't take days to know that we are going to fuck before you leave here. Why waste time when we can fuck for several days instead of a day."

It amazed me how he went from kind of reserved to a nigga in the streets. He bent down kissed then licked my neck. Goosebumps popped up all over my body as I imagined him licking other spots on me. I pulled away from him and walked into the bathroom. After that, I felt my juices coming down my legs, and I had to take care it. I walked out of the bathroom, and Bryce was still waiting for me.

"Come on ma let me show you how to tear down a mall. Since you're coming home with me until you leave, I might as well sponsor your shopping. We have a lot a shit to take care of this week." I walked past him to Bailey and Marcus who was standing on the other side of the door before turning around.

"Thanks, but no thanks. I can sponsor my own shopping spree and who said I was going home with you."

"It can be voluntarily or involuntarily; either way you will be with me for the rest of the week." Bryce left me standing there with my mouth open I turned to Bailey.

"Don't look at me. Shit, I'm going to help him kidnap your ass."

✹ 7 ✹

BRYCE

I glanced at Takhiya sitting comfortably in the passenger seat like she belonged next me. She turned in her seat looking at me

"Why me?" I stroked my beard.

"Why not you, ma?"

"From the car you're driving, and the money you spent at the mall, I can tell you can have any female you want out here. So again, why me?" I kept my eyes on the road.

"I really can't say why it's you, but what I can say is that you're the first female in a long time that I've been interested than putting more than just my dick in. Don't take that the wrong way either because I still want to put my dick in you, I just want your company before and after that." I could tell she was at a lost for words for a second. When she arched her eyebrow at me, I knew it was over.

"So, you were willing to kidnap me and go to jail for attraction?" I turned to look at her

"Hell yeah, I would've snatched your ass from your hotel room and drug your ass out the door kicking and screaming. As for jail, mutha-fuckas in there would have been blind and mute to the shit. If I would have had to kidnap you, you wouldn't have been going home until I decided to let you go." She took her seat belt off turning completely towards me.

"What type of shit is that? You act more like a common thug, than the businessman you portrayed in public. As a matter fact, what do you do?" I smiled at her.

"I indulge in a little of everything, but my main focus of work is taking over companies that are not run properly and in order. I reconstruct some things and then give them to one of my people to run. In return, I get a small percentage of what comes." Takhiya stared at me for so long I felt like she was burning a hole in through me.

We pulled up to my house, and I got out the car opened the door for her to get out. I then grabbed all the bags and opened the door to the house. Takhiya stepped in the house, and her mouth dropped.

"Who lives here with you?" I sat the bags down on the table.

"My five-year-old daughter, but she's at camp for the next two weeks. Would you like something to drink?"

"Yes please, some water would be nice."

I walked to the kitchen got two bottles of water and came back into the living room to Takhiya bending over. Her ass was so round that I could see her cheeks hanging from under the little ass sundress she had on. My dick got brick hard. I wanted nothing more than to slide right in her and make her scream with every stroke I would give her. I walked a little closer and saw she had no panties on. I walked up behind her dropped to knees and stuck my tongue right into her pussy.

From the moans she let out, I knew she loved this type of nasty shit. I moved my tongue in her and used one hand to play with her clit and the other to pull her back to me. Her pussy started clenching on my tongue as she got wetter and juices flowed down into my mouth. Her knees began to buckle a little, but I held onto her tighter. I brought my tongue from her pussy to her clit and pushed two of my fingers into her. I curled my fingers into her, and when I found the right spot, she was screaming my name and squirting all down my face.

When she turned around to me and started licking her juices off my face, I knew this was going to be one hell of a week. I pulled a condom out of my pocket unzipped my pants and walked her backwards to the table. Once her ass hit the dining room table, I lifted her on there ripped the spaghetti straps to her dress, pulled it down, and put her titties in my mouth one at a time. As she moaned my name, in on quick motion, I was balls deep into her. I gripped her hips and to pull her closer to me. I put both of her legs on my shoulders to make sure I hit everything in her. I bit her leg, and she started coming on my dick, but it was when she started rolling her hips and working her muscles, I knew that I would have to kidnap this bitch for real.

Takhiya was taking the dick like a champ, and I was nowhere near a small man. When she wet my stomach from coming, and her pussy put a death grip on my dick, I knew it was the end of that round. I pulled her off the table.

"Come on, the only time you will come out of the room today is to eat."

She stopped like she was a little hesitant.

"What's the problem, ma?"

"I just think you should know..." I cut her short.

"Unless you have an STD that I can catch through the condom, I don't need to know shit. This is a week of nothing but fun. I could care less about your past, present, or future."

She looked down at the floor, and then followed me to the bar. I poured us a glass of Hennessy, and we walked to the room. When we got there, I went to the bed, pulled my chrome desert eagles from under both pillows, and watched her eyes get big,

"What you've never seen a gun before?" She walked over to me and sat on the bed.

"It's not that. I'm just trying to figure out what type of businessman needs two desert eagles under his pillow."

I stood there intrigued because she knew what type of gun it was and what I thought was fear at first was only curiosity. She turned the glass of Hennessy up that I gave her and drained the glass.

"These are my babies, and I keep them close," I stated, putting them in my nightstand.

Takhiya walked over to me pushing me on the bed. She pulled my dick out and popped it in her mouth. Her shit was sloppy wet. She went all the way down on my shit and then did this thing with her tongue that had me about to bust right then. She kept her mouth wet and it felt like she didn't have not one tooth in her mouth. She got a fire shot, and God himself blessed her with that mouth.

❧

I WOKE UP TO TAKHIYA STRADDLING ME ON MY DICK AND TAKING me for the ride of my life. After she came, I turned her over and tore her ass up.

"Throw on something; I need to go check on the club."

She got up and walked to the shower, and I checked out the booty shorts and baby tee that she was going to put on and put it back in her bag. I put one of the bags of clothes that I had got for her and sat it on the bed with some oversized Chanel shades to match the outfit in the bag, and the shoes were next to it. Takhiya walked out the bathroom about an hour in a half later, and her hair was bone straight and hung to the middle of her back. Her makeup was light but perfect, and her lips had a little shine to them. She picked up the bags on the bed.

"Where are the clothes that I laid out?" I put on my Creed cologne.

"In the bag with the rest of the clothes you bought yesterday."

I walked out of the room and went downstairs to wait on her. The last thing I wanted to do was to have a disagreement with her. Today I wanted chill, take her to see my hometown, take her out to eat dinner, and then come home and eat her pussy. She walked down the stairs and had on the Chanel sundress I had got her. I swear I wanted to bend that ass over right there. That would have to wait; we had business to take care of.

We walked out the door, and I had the Land Rover sitting out front, I opened the door and helped her get in.

"I guess business is excellent for you." She rolled her eyes and smirked at me. I pulled off before I started talking.

"I got something planned for us today, but business first." I turned the music up, and we rode in silence all the way to the club.

As soon as I opened the door to the club, a naked Jasmine greeted us. She had her back turned to us and the six inches Jimmy Choos she had on had her ass commanding my attention. I cleared my throat twice before she turned around and saw that someone was with me. Takhiya stood there with a smile on her face, as Jasmine became flustered and turned red in front of us.

"I didn't know you were bringing someone with you today." Jasmine covered herself with her arms as she turned to walk away. As she did, her ass made waves from jiggling as she picked up her pace. Takhiya laughed once Jasmine was out of earshot.

"What the hell Bryce, you get greeted at the door with pussy? Is this a strip club or something?" I laughed with her

"Naw ma, it's just a regular club. Jasmine is my assistant manager."

"Yeah, I see she assist you with the pussy too."

I continued to laugh as I showed her around the club. Once Jasmine had on her clothes, she came back out, apologized, and introduced herself. Once we left, I showed Takhiya what my city had to offer and took her out for a late lunch. We kept our conversation light and just really enjoyed each other's company. She told me about how she just broke up with her dude, and Miami was like a celebration trip for her. I didn't want to get into details with her because while she was sitting next to me, that nigga wasn't important. One thing I knew she wasn't doing at this moment was fucking that nigga. I was going to do my best so that when she got back if she did decide to fuck him, he would know for sure someone else had been knee deep in her pussy.

I pulled up to the house and saw a car sitting in my driveway, so I pulled my nine out of pants. Once I got closer, I put it back up but I knew all hell was finna break loose.

"Shit! Fuck! Shit!" Takhiya looked at me like I had gone crazy.

"Who is that?" she asked as we pulled up on the car.

"I'm his fucking wife bitch, who are you?" Takhiya turned and looked at me like I had fucked up.

"You bastard you're married, and you had me sleeping in the bed that you and your wife share?" I shook my head, but before I could answer Takhiya, Olivia smacked the shit out of me.

"You had this hoe in our bed? You a dirty motherfucka, how the fuck did I end up with a low down ass nigga like you?"

Takhiya walked in the house, and when she came back out, she had changed out of the clothes I had gotten her and into some shorts and t-shirt.

"Takhiya, she is not my wife we have been divorced for four years, I swear." Takhiya looked up at me from her phone.

"We haven't been together since she left me at the hospital with our daughter Justice the day after she was born." Olivia stepped between us.

"How dare you stand in front of me and lie like that. I'm an excellent mother to our child. You know what Bryce you got me fucked up and so does this fat bitch right here. Hoe, you need to start walking away before I beat your ass." Takhiya turned to Olivia.

"You may beat his ass if he allows you too, but bitch I'm not taking any ass whipping her. You need to talk to your husband." Olivia stepped up to her.

"Bitch, you have no idea who I am, do you?" Takhiya pushed Olivia out of her face.

"No bitch, but I know who you ain't my motherfuckin' mother." Olivia charged towards Takhiya. I lifted her off her feet just as Takhiya's Uber was pulling up to the front door. The driver pulled off, and I put Olivia down.

"Damn, why do you always have to fuck up my life?"

Instead of answering, Olivia started hitting me. I was past tired of her shit over these years. I wrapped my hands around her neck and started squeezing her shit. Her eyes turned red and watered as they bulged as if they were about to pop out of the sockets. She started gasping for air, and I squeezed even harder, hoping I end this bitch life today. Suddenly, I felt someone snatching me back, and Olivia fell to the ground trying to catch her breath.

"Man, what the fuck is wrong with you? Are you trying to kill her?" I walked up the steps to the house as I shouted to my oldest brother Pierre.

"Hell yeah."

8

BAILEY

I was laying on my back while this fine ass nigga was on his knees giving me some fye head. He had me trying to get away from him but wanting to stay in that one spot at the same time. If every nigga in Miami gives head like this, I will transfer jobs and become a permanent resident. I had to be on my third orgasm when Takhiya walked in my room fuming. I tried to push dude that I couldn't remember his name for shit up, but he was so into eating my cake he hadn't noticed my girl walking in.

"Nigga, do you not see my bitch in here? Have some fucking manners." He lifted his head up looking at me.

"What? She can join in; I don't mind." I rolled my eyes laughing at how serious he was as Takhiya walked back into her room.

"Nigga, get out my damn room." He got up, put on his clothes, and walked out the door. I went to shower real quick before going to talk to Khiya.

I soaped up washing off in a hurry and went to Khiya's room. She was lying on the bed with a cold towel on her forehead, and a glass in her hand that I knew had Hennessy in it at one point.

"What happened now? I just knew that nigga was gonna fuck you into a coma, and you wouldn't remember Quan dirty ass by the time we go home." Takhiya held her glass up to me without opening her eyes.

"Bitch, what didn't happen? First, we went to his club and was welcomed at the door by a naked bitch in some bad ass Jimmy Choos. He showed me around town, and we went to an expensive ass restaurant for a late lunch. Despite the shit that happened that morning, I just knew I was going to get to the house and get the dick. Then, this nigga's wife shows up at the house acting a damn fool."

My mouth dropped I usually have something to say, but nothing came out. After my mouth started to dry out from being open, I shook my head.

"You mean to tell me that after all that shit about kidnapping you, Bryce is married?" Takhiya moved the towel from her head and walked to the bar.

"With children." I fell back on the bed.

"Did you at least get the dick yesterday?" She poured herself another drink.

"Bitch, did I. That man busted it wide open then kissed it to make it feel better. Why the fuck you think I'm standing here drinking so much?" I raised my eyebrow at her.

"Because you're a fucking alcoholic."

I got up to walk out the room, and Takhiya threw a pillow at me.

"Naw hoe, who was that nigga in there that offered me a three-some?" I walked back in the room knowing that I wasn't going anywhere too soon.

"When you find out who he is let me know."

We both laughed I was dead ass though. I came here to have fun and fuck enough to hold me over till the next trip not remember a nigga name. I was at the beach yesterday, and buddy told me that he was a pussy connoisseur, and I wanted to find out if it was true. I led his ass right to my room, and that nigga ate my pussy like a champ. Evidently, he loved it because he came back this morning for seconds, thirds, and fourths. Takhiya looked at me.

"What happened to Marcus fine ass?"

"He tried to pull the same kidnap shit with me that Bryce pulled with you. When I told him that I would cut and stick everything that came way and pulled out my knife, he asked me how did I get a knife bigger than me on the plane. I told him, and he called me crazy and hasn't been around since, but he has texted me a couple of times to make sure I was cool." Takhiya laughed at me.

"I can only imagine where you hide that knife." She doubled over laughing at me.

"So, is that it with you and Bryce? I mean we're leaving next week. You don't have to see him anymore after that."

"Bailey, it has been a lot of fucked up shit I've done in my life that I have to hold myself accountable for. I'm already going to have trouble getting into heaven; I won't put willingly sleeping with a married man on a never-ending highway to hell list."

I understood where she was coming from. I couldn't act like I didn't my girl had been through a lot of shit. If you asked ten people to share the burden of her life thus far, every one of them would say no. I'm her best friend, and I would've said no. That shit takes a strong ass person to make it through like she did.

"Says the bitch holding the fifth of Hennessy in her hand. Bitch, you can't be holy with a bottle of spirits."

"Fuck you, Bailey!" I walked over to my door.

"Ummhum." She was just mad because I made valid ass points, but she had definitely made one too. I know motherfuckas think I'm an asshole for that statement, but I'd rather take a little anger from her than to have her reflecting on her life and feeling sorry for herself.

I got back to my room, and my text was going off I looked at the phone.

Marcus: *What you on today?*
Me: *I don't have anything planned. What's up?*
Marcus: *Is Takhiya with you?*
Me: *Yeah why?*
Marcus: *Grab her and y'all meet me down in the lobby in an hour and a half.*
Me: *Ok.*
Marcus: *Wear a swimsuit.*

I didn't know what he had planned, but I knew it had something to do with Bryce. I went back to Takhiya room.

"Get dressed, but put your swimsuit on under your clothes." I was walking back to the room.

"Where are we going? I turned back to her.

"Swimming." I went back to the room and got ready.

An hour later, Takhiya came into my room dressed in a red two-piece bra and high waist short swimsuit. I looked at my friend, and she was really pretty, she was curvaceous with very little stomach and not a stretch mark in sight. I smiled at her and handed her the drink I had ready for her.

"This is to fucking someone else's man." She looked at me crazy.

"Bitch, other women been fucking your man for the longest, so it's time to return the favor to somebody's nigga." She laughed at me, and we talked shit for a minute before it was time to go downstairs.

Marcus pulled up in a Mercedes truck rolling down the window.

"Y'all gonna get in."

I flipped him off and got in the truck getting comfortable, Marcus looked delicious with his swim trunks on with no shirt. I mean his green eyes had hints of hazel in them his hair was braided straight to the back. Even though he was leaning forward, you could still see the definition of his six-pack. He was fine as hell, but it was something about him that was brotherly. He was cool, but I couldn't force myself to want to fuck with him on that level.

I'm the type of woman that knows it takes a special type of man to fuck with me on that level. I guess you can say that I'm scared of love. I'm afraid of loving someone the way Takhiya loved Quan. I'm a little off already, so I think I might go fucking crazy if my nigga did half the shit Quan has done. Not mental institution crazy, but tie that nigga to the bed and set it on fire crazy, or come in the house shooting at they ass crazy. My problem is that I'm scared of the unknown and love isn't something that isn't guaranteed. Therefore, I fuck who want, and after that, they have to go about their business. If it's good, we might get some months.

Once a nigga starts showing feelings, they have to go. A lot of people have the game backwards. They swear that women are the ones on that catch feelings quicker, but men need that connection with women more than we do. I realized I'm just not the relationship type of girl and I'm ok with that; getting a nut every now and then is fine with me.

We pulled up to one of the beaches got out the car and walked down the beach. We got to a spot that people were taking rides on dolphins, and Bryce came out of nowhere.

"Takhiya, you didn't want to listen earlier, but Olivia and I are not married. She wants to act like we are, but doesn't want to accept her own child. I don't even know why she popped at my house. That has never happened before, and it won't happen again. Let me make this up to you." Takhiya turned her head and started walking away. I looked at Bryce.

"Yo, you know that nice shit doesn't work on women with attitudes, right?" He took off behind her.

❦

I LOOKED AT MYSELF IN THE MIRROR, AND I CAN SAY I LOOKED damn good. I rubbed my fingers through my low cut to feather my curls. My black bodycon dress hugged my curves just right. The back of it plunged down to my ass, and then the dress cuffed right under it. I touched up my nude lip gloss enhanced my caramel skin and made sure my face was beat to the gods. I walked out the bathroom and put on my five-inch stilettos silver Louboutin stilettos that still didn't add much of a difference to my almost five feet height. I knocked on Takhiya's door to see if she was ready to step out.

Marcus and Bryce had been getting on my nerves making sure we came to the grand opening of Mariano's. We had to push our flight plans back one day, just to go. Takhiya stepped into my room with a Chanel jumpsuit on that Bryce had bought for her. It was all black, and it had rips going across her chest to her navel and from her hips to her thighs down the front. Her four-inch red Chanel peep-toe stilettos brought out the thin red chain that hung across her hips and a red clutch purse that matched her shoes perfectly. Her makeup was flawless, and the red lipstick she had on was everything. She finished it off with platinum diamond studs in her ears, and her hair was bone straight

"Slay bitch, slay." Takhiya laughed at me.

"Naw this ain't shit compared to what you have on." I did a little spin for her to get a good look at me.

We got to the lobby, a driver was waiting for us. Bryce and Marcus spared no expense on us. We got in the black on black Escalade limo, and there was a bucket of champagne with two glasses sitting on top of the cooler. These niggas really knew how to show females a good time. I was loving it too. It was a breath of fresh air compared to the how the men are in the Chi.

We got to the club getting out at the front door, the line was wrapped around the building, and I was glad I didn't have to wait. Takhiya and I walked up to the guard as he was removing the ropes, and I felt all eyes on us. Hoes was rolling their eyes and smacking their lips. I even heard someone ask someone "who the fuck are they supposed to be?" I laughed a little because it was a lot of shit that came to my head on how to answer that question. The main one I thought was not the bitch waiting in line. There was no need to begin my night with fucking up a hating ass hoe, so I kept it moving into the club.

We walked in once my eyes adjusted to the lights and smoke; this club was banging. A huge bar sat in the middle of the floor, and the roof of it was all glass. Everything in here was marble or some kind of granite except for the floors. There were black, red, and silver leather couches and chairs. I guess the best word to describe everything was elegant with a twist. The party was lit, the bass was booming, and people were all over the floor. I guess you could consider this grand opening a success and the party had only been going for about two hours.

We started moving through the thick crowd going towards the bar, and the beat to my favorite song came on, I pulled Takhiya to the middle of the floor with me. We both starting dancing to Drake's *"One Dance."*

By the time Drake's words came out of the speakers, we were both on the floor rolling and making our ass shake from twerking.

Baby I like your style
Grips on your legs
Front way, back way

YOU KNOW THAT I DON'T PLAY
Streets not safe
But I never run away
Even when I'm away

OT, OT IS NEVER MUCH LOVE WHEN WE GO OT
I pray to make it back in one piece
I pray, I pray
That's why I need a one dance

GOT THE HENNESSY IN MY HAND
One more time 'fore I go
I have powers taking ahold on me
I need a one dance
Got the Hennessy in my hand
One more time 'fore I go
I have powers taking ahold on me

SOME GUY CAME UP BEHIND ME, AND TAKHIYA STEPPED BACK AS WE put on a show for everyone. Once they changed the song, I turned to look at dude. He looked just like Marcus without the green eyes, but sexier. I thanked him for the dance and just as quick as he came, he left. Takhiya and I walked over to the bar as Bryce and Marcus were walking up to us.

"Ladies, it's nice to see that you finally made it here," Marcus said giving us both a kiss on Cheek.

I just rolled my eyes at him and let the remark slide, while he was checking me out.

"You guys have a nice little spot; I'm glad we stayed for the open-ing," I said while trying to get the bartenders attention.

"We got a booth over there in the corner; they will get you what-

47

ever you want." I nodded my head at Marcus and turned to walk towards the booth when he pulled me back out to the dance floor. I looked at Takhiya, but she was with Bryce, and I knew she would be cool.

"See you in the booth. Let me show Marcus a thing or two on this floor." Takhiya waved her hand at me gesturing to go head, and I followed Marcus out to the floor.

Marcus and I hit the dance floor and were out there for two songs before shots rang out in the club. Marcus pulled me one way, and I ran in the opposite direction to the bar where I had left Takhiya, I frantically looked around and didn't see her. I felt someone pull me down to the floor as several more shots went off.

9

TAKHIYA

Bryce and I watched Marcus and Bailey cut up on the dance floor for a few minutes before walking over towards the booth. He had pulled close to him like I was his prize possession. I love the fact that he makes me feel like I'm the only woman in the room.

"You look beautiful in that outfit. I knew when I saw it that your curves would fill it out perfectly."

I was smiling and blushing so damn hard I couldn't even thank him for the compliment. I returned his compliment because he was fine as hell in his all-black Armani suit with a white shirt, and he smelled so good. I knew once the night was over he was coming to the hotel with me. He had my pussy so wet just from looking at me that I wanted to take his ass down in the middle of the dance floor. My mind was full of all the freaky shit I wanted to do to him before I left tomorrow. I wanted his dick to stand up at the thought of me. I was ready to brand his dick with my pussy. I knew that tonight would be all that we have left, and I'm damn sure going to make it a night for him to remember.

He pulled me towards him to go to the booth. We had made it halfway through the thick crowd. I was just about tell Bryce how much I appreciate everything he'd done when I heard people started screaming. Bryce and I turned around to see guns aimed towards us. Bryce stepped in front of me before shots rang out all over the club. Bryce pulled me down to the floor. People were running everywhere, and some people were on the floor screaming from being trampled over. As the room broke out into chaos, I tried to get Bryce to crawl towards the back of the club, but he wasn't moving. I felt stickiness all over my body. I looked down at myself, and I was covered in blood. I crouched down and pulled Bryce over into a corner.

"KHIYA!" I heard Bailey screaming my name. I looked around, and she was running around hysterical looking for me.

"Hush and come over here." She ran over to me and looked down at Bryce's white dress shirt covered in blood.

"WE NEED TO GET OUT OF HERE."

I kept my hands on Bryce's chest, knowing that I couldn't leave him in the middle of this shit. The only reason he was shot in the first place is because he jumped in front of me. I owe this nigga my life, and I will risk mine to make sure he pulls through this. I guess this is the real definition of a ride or die bitch because I was stuck to this nigga at the moment and wasn't moving for shit.

"No, I just can't leave him like this." He was losing so much blood

The gunshots stopped, and I took in my surroundings but didn't stand up.

"Bailey, I need you to see if you can find Marcus." She looked at me I could tell she was scared, and she looked at me sideways.

"You know I wouldn't put you in harm's way. We need some help." She stared at me for a couple of seconds, and then she crawled away to do as I asked her.

I looked down at Bryce.

"Just hold on for me baby. You got this." He looked at me with his hazel eyes low then they closed completely."

Used my right hand to check his pulse, he was still alive for now, but I couldn't help but wonder what the hell was taking Bailey so long. I kept talking to him telling him it was going to be ok. I didn't want to lose him like this. We were supposed to say our goodbyes after having sex all night, not with him bleeding all over me at his club. I closed my eyes and prayed that he pulled through this when I heard a gun cock behind me. I just knew this was going to be my last time talking to God on earth. I envisioned meeting Bryce at the pearly gates and us holding hands walking to tell God how we ended up in front of him for judgment day. Laquan came to my mind. I knew he would miss me but would find comfort in some random bitch pussy. I said another prayer hoping this wasn't my last day on earth.

"Get the fuck off my brother, or I'll put a bullet in your head before you can blink your eyes." I knew the man behind me wasn't Marcus, and I knew if I took my hands off Bryce he would die.

"Go ahead, but if I move your brother dies anyway, just let me help him." The guy walked to the other side of Bryce and me, keeping his gun pointed at my head. He looked down at us and tears formed in his eyes. He turned his head and looked back down at us.

Bailey finally made it back over to me with Marcus in tow. I exhaled a breath as Marcus stared at his brother like he was crazy and snatched the gun from his hand.

"Pierre, what the hell is wrong with you? You're going to kill the person that's trying to help our brother stay alive?" Pierre snapped out of his trance and pulled out his phone talking to someone saying we were on the way. He turned to Marcus.

"Find Marcell we need his help, and you on the floor if you let him die you will meet him in death, do you understand me?" Marcus shook his head at Pierre and ran off. Bailey stood in front of Pierre, glaring at him. Their brother Marcell ran over to us, Pierre and Marcell picked Bryce up and ran to a truck, putting him in the back seat. Pierre looked at me.

"Get in and what I said still stands; keep him alive." I got in the back of the truck after looking around to see Bailey and Marcus. I held on to Bryce and continued to pray for him.

"Who the fuck is this bitch, and why is she in the car with us?" Marcell asked while giving me the evil eye. I rolled my eyes at his rude ass and ignored him.

"What the fuck it looks like she's doing, nigga? Without her, Bryce dies. Does your ignorant ass want that happen? We have too much to lose if Bryce leaves this earth; he's the head of this family. If he leaves that leaves us in a fucked up predicament, think before you speak sometimes. If that bitch takes her hands off of him over your stupid ass, I'm going to hurt you." Pierre was pissed off.

"My name is Takhiya." They had been slanging that bitch word a little too loosely for me, and I was tired of that shit. My mama didn't name me that shit and they needed to know that. Marcell turned around to look at me.

"Bitch, do you know who we are? I can say whatever the fuck I want. Who the hell is gone stop me from calling you a bitch? We run this fucking city. One bitch ain't finna stop me from speaking my mind." He stared me down.

"Nigga turn your stupid ass around before you kill all of us." Pierre smacked the back of Marcell's head.

☙❧

IT WAS TOUCH AND GO TO GET BRYCE TO SOME HOUSE THAT THEY said the doctor was. We all sat in a basement in silence as their brother Marcell huffed and paced the floors. He finally turned to Pierre to get what he had on his chest off. He glared at me.

"Why the fuck is this fat bitch still doing here?" He pointed at me.

Bailey shot up out of her chair walking up to Marcell.

"I would think you would be more appreciative and respectful of the fat bitch that just helped save your fucking brother's life, asshole." Her head barely reached his chest as she jabbed her index finger into him.

Marcell moved closer to Bailey pushing his chest out trying to intimidate her, and that was the wrong move to make. Bailey stepped back and reached her hand up and smacked the hell out Marcell. We all laughed at them. Marcus got out of his seat and pulled Bailey back to the chair. After all the action was over, I looked between Marcus and Marcell. They were a reflection of each other, but when Marcell was trying to boss Marcus around earlier, I heard him say that he was the older.

We stayed in that house for three days, and it was touch and go with Bryce most of the time. I didn't want to leave the house until I knew that he would make it out of here. Once he was awake and stable, Marcell took us to the hotel to pack up. The ride back was a rough one. I thought Bailey was going to rip Marcell a new asshole. What they couldn't explain to me though was what happened when they took so long to get us some clothes and food the second night we were at the house. When I asked about it, the look on Bailey's face was priceless, and Marcell just looked at me and turned his head.

One thing that this trip to Miami did teach me was that life is too short to not be with the one you love. LaQuan has done some fucked up shit over the years, but if nothing else I know he loves more than anything. Six hours later we walked into my house. I knew Quan had been here because the house was spotless compared to the way I left it. Bailey and I sat our bags down and walked right to the living room, laying across the furniture reflecting on our vacation.

"If I knew then what I know now, we could've stayed in Chicago for the shit we went through out there," Bailey said as she kicked her shoes off her feet.

Before I could get a response out of my mouth, I heard Quan ass moaning loud as hell.

"I know the fuck this nigga ain't." I jumped to my feet and walked slowly up the stairs with Bailey on my heels. The door to our room was cracked, I peeped through the door and bile came to my throat.

❧ 10 ❧

LAQUAN

I was in the middle of making my dick touch the back of a motherfucka's throat, Takhiya had me convulsing while she was sucking my shit. I have never tried to snatch my dick out of someone's mouth before, but I couldn't help myself. This head game had me feeling like a bitch, trying to pull away and moaning loud as hell. It just the way I like it too; her mouth was all wet but not sloppy, using her tongue on the tip. When she deep throated, she did this thing with her throat muscles that made me want to bust every time. I could tell the trip to Miami had done us some good and that she missed daddy's dick because she was doing shit she had never done before. Her head game was always the best I've ever had, but she has stepped her game up.

The first thing that came to my mind after that was who dick had this bitch been sucking Miami? This bitch really has me fucked up to think she can just walk in and do some new shit and think I'm not going beat her ass for it. I moaned aloud again pulled Takhiya's head down to me and felt a fade. *I know this bitch ain't cut her hair?* I opened my eyes to see my nigga Jason between my legs, and my eyes bulged out my head. I couldn't believe this shit, my best friend, and my right hand that I have been knowing since fifth grade is on his fucking knees with my dick in his mouth. I was past mad, and all I felt was fuck rage. I started seeing red, and I was ready to put a bullet in this nigga's head.

"What you doing, nigga?" I tried to push his head off me, but this nigga had the Jaws of Life suctioned on my shit. I started swinging on him, sending blows to his head and this nigga just kept sucking.

"Relax nigga; you know you want this." Jason stopped just long enough to say but kept a tight grip on my junk.

"I don't want this gay ass shit. Nigga, get off of me." I tried to get up, but it felt like a boulder was holding me down. I did the only thing I could think to and that was to start swinging again. I couldn't believe this shit I was being raped in my own fucking house by my right hand. I tried to block out from my mind that this shit felt good. I felt violated and like I was finna bust at the same time. I kept punching at him, and he kept sucking like it wasn't doing shit to him. This had to be one fucked up dream; this nigga had more bodies than me. We had taken bitches down together in the same room, and he has a whole bitch with kids. This can't be life right now.

I was in the midst of busting of still trying to push this nigga head back when our phones started ringing out back to back. He let go of my dick, and I rolled off the bed hitting the floor, I tried to stand up, but my knees were wobbly. I needed to get to my gun because I was definitely finna fuck up this white carpet with his blood. My phone rang out again I went to grab it, but Jason was already yelled out and ran out the door. I looked up at the door, and there was my baby and Bailey looking at me. Bailey had her phone facing me. I got off the floor and took a couple of steps towards them when I stumbled back to the floor. Takhiya had grabbed Jason up and was hitting him with the bat that she kept in the hall closet.

I got up and stumbled towards Bailey to grab her phone, and she took off down the stairs. I stepped to go after her and Takhiya dropped the bat in front of me, and I went tumbling down the steps. I laid at the bottom of the stairs on my back when my boy damn near stepped on me trying to get out the door. Takhiya was right behind him, but pointing my gun at my head.

"You know I should put this bullet in your head for making me look like a fool for all these years. Nigga I gave you my all, and this is how you do me? You had me out heismaning these niggas while you were fucking with hoes left and right now you fucking your best friend. I've been through hell fighting hoes and damn near losing my fucking job because of your bitches coming there to start shit when all along I should've been fighting you and Jason bitch ass. Y'all ain't shit but some down low, homo, thug ass motherfuckas. Get out of my house and don't come back."

Her hand was shaking, and I didn't want no mistakes in this motherfucka, so I got up off the floor and held my head down.

"Baby just let me explain, this shit really wasn't what it looked like. I can..." Takhiya cut me off.

"You disgust me, just go!"

I looked at her and nothing but hurt and resentment showed in her eyes. At that moment, I knew I had lost my baby forever. I didn't attempt to grab anything out the house, but the jogging pants and gym shoes that was in the room on the first level. I put my shit on as I was coming out of the room. Takhiya was standing there with my phone in one hand and the gun in the other.

"You might and might not want this. You tricked me, but I guarantee you won't trick the world. I made sure to tag your mama too. She should be happy you're not with a crack head like me anymore." I grabbed the phone and opened my Facebook app to see Jason on his knees and trying to push his head back. Looking at the video, it looked like I was pushing his head down to me.

I looked back at my baby she still had the gun in her hand pointing at me as I walked out the door. Bailey was leaning on Takhiya's truck with a smirk on her face. I moved to go towards her, but Takhiya cleared her throat, and I walked pass Bailey glaring at her.

My boy Jason came by the house, to pick me up for a party we were stepping out to. Normally I would drive myself, but when I got to my truck after Patrice pulled off on me, it wouldn't start. Jason came into the house he gave me two mollies for the night I threw them back and drank the rest of the D'usse I had in my glass to wash it down. I threw him the remote control and went upstairs texted Takhiya, pulled out my clothes, and took a shower. I walked out the bathroom, sprayed on some Clive Christian for men. I walked over to my dresser to put on some deodorant and got dizzy.

I walked over to my bed and laid on my back just to get myself together. The whole time I didn't know that nigga was on me. I had fallen asleep and was dreaming that Takhiya had come home and was happy to see me. In my dream, she had kissed me all over my body, then gave me a slow and dragging kiss on the lips before she took my dick in her mouth and sucked my soul through it, only for me to wake up to my nigga with his mouth on my shit.

I continued to walk the streets trying to make it to my destination, and my phone continued to go off. Everyone that I thought I could call was blasting me, I was in a fucked up predicament, and it didn't seem like it was going to get any better. I had two bitches to thank for that — Patrice for fucking up the engine in my car, and Bailey for fucking up life. I will never be respected out here again, and when I get my hands on Jason, his mama won't be able to identify his body.

❧ II ❧

BRYCE

"**W**hat I want to know is how did the motherfuckas get into my club, try to fucking kill me, and damn near succeed? Where the fuck were my brothers when I needed you most?" I punched the wall and turned around looking at my brother Pierre for an explanation.

"Nigga, we were getting shot at just like your ass was," he retorted with his chest out getting closer to me.

Our youngest brother Marcus walked between us being the peacemaker as usual. I pushed him out the way and walked back up to Pierre. I love my brother, but he tends to forget that I'm the one he has to answer to in the end. When everything first started out, I tried to split most responsibility evenly between the four of us. Pierre let the power go to his head and killed a whole lot of people on one of his power trips. In the end, I had to answer for all that shit and get everything back in order.

I bought his ass back to earth real quick. Since he wanted to be trigger-happy, I put him in charge of our security. At first, he wasn't too happy with the position he played, but I had to let him know if outsiders came in it could cause more harm than good. For the most part, he has been on point, but I just couldn't understand how I was almost killed with him being the best at what he does. After being over the family for so long, I finally understand my father's reasons for making me the head of the family.

Pierre just isn't too bright; that nigga was missing a couple of screws. Marcell is a beast and will never be the type to think things through. He is the type to shoot first and fuck the questions. If a motherfucka that wasn't family asked him about it, he would kill they ass too. And, Marcus was all about the hoes and clothes. Together we are more than a force to be reckoned with, only under my strict guidance though.

"You know if Papi were alive, he wouldn't honor this shit." Our brother Marcell got off the couch and walked to me.

"If Papi were alive he wouldn't want us arguing with each other. He would want us to go after the motherfuckas that tried to take us out. Now chill, we need to figure this shit out."

Pierre and I looked at each other and sat down. Out of the Mariano brothers, it was four of us. Pierre being the oldest at thirty, then myself at two years his junior. Marcell, the hothead, is three years younger than I am, then you have Marcus who was exactly nine months younger than Marcell. We always joked that mommy gave it up to papi right after Marcell's delivery. Everyone one in the family called them the Irish twins. The crazy part is that they were almost identical, except Marcell has our mother's brown eyes, and Marcus has our father's green eyes.

Our roots run deep into Italy from our father's side of the family and being half black only made us have to prove ourselves even more to the families. For that reason, people always tried us. I still feel some type of way about the death of our parents. Three years ago, they went on a trip to Italy and never made it back home because their plane went down on the way back. My father had all of his wishes in his will, which made me the head of the family because of me having a level head and being business savvy. Deep down I knew Pierre was pissed that he wasn't over us. He was great at what he did which was protecting us, but when it came to business, he wasn't interested. I looked over at my brothers, and we all have come a long way from three years ago.

"Marcell, were you able to get the information I asked you for?" Marcell looked at me shaking his head before responding.

"I'm working on it bro; you have to give me a little more time." I narrowed my eyes at him.

"How much more time you need, it's been three months?" He stood up walking towards the door before speaking.

"Like I said I need more time." Marcell walked out of the door, slamming it hard.

I had laid in the bed at one of our doctor's houses for two and half months. Before I was even well, I asked about Takhiya. I couldn't get her out of my head. She was the last face I saw before I blacked out the day I got shot. I wanted her to be the first face I saw when I woke up, but my brothers told me she had gone home. I owed her my life. I've never had anyone to put their life in danger to save mine except my brothers.

The least I could do was thank her properly for saving me. It's crazy how she was only here for a little over a week, and I feel like I have known her a lifetime. The last thing I thought I wanted in my life was a woman. Women are some sneaky, lying, money hungry, conniving ass creatures. Takhiya is different; she could care less about my money, and she's to brutally honest to lie and be sneaky. he's a little rough around the edges, but I know I can make her shine like the diamond she is. She would be the perfect fit for a mob boss like myself.

"Yo Bryce, you cool?" Marcus yelled from across the room breaking my thought.

"Yeah I'm good; I just need a little air."

I stood up fixing my suit jacket and looking at the difference in the way my youngest brother dressed compared to myself and smiled. Three years ago, that was me in Robin jeans and Gucci gym shoes. I walked out of the office leaving Pierre and Marcus in there talking. My mind was on two things— who tried to make my ass maggot food and how the fuck did they let Takhiya leave without getting her information? I couldn't understand what's taking so long for them to get this information for me when I'm a damn mob boss.

My phone vibrated in my pocket. Once I show the name of the texter, I knew it couldn't be good. I laid my head back on the couch, closing my eyes trying to gather my thoughts when my five-year-old Justice ran into the room and jumped in my lap. I loved my baby more than life itself and missed her so much, but she finds the finest times to come talk to her daddy. I sat up giving her a hug and kiss on the cheek, ignoring the throbbing pain of a headache that started.

"Hi, daddy!" I looked at her and smiled.

"Hey daddy's girl, how's your day going?" Justice looked at me ready to tell me all of the things that happened in her little world.

Justice's mouth ran a mile a minute. I missed baby during the months that I was down, she was the reason that I fought so hard to stay alive. After talking to my baby girl for thirty minutes, I sent her to play with her toys and pulled out my phone.

Olivia: *My father wants to talk to you.*

I didn't even respond to her. Pierre and Mr. Romano had some bad blood from back in the day. Pierre had talked my brother Marcus into poisoning the old man dogs after he had fucked Mr. Romano's oldest daughter five ways from Sunday. Mr. Romano swore his daughter was a saint and virgin, and Pierre told him a virgin doesn't suck dick and swallow like she was born in a brothel. To say Mr. Romano was pissed was an understatement; he tried his hand at beating Pierre's ass and was sadly mistaken.

One month later, Mr. Romano came to my dad ranting about Pierre getting his innocent daughter pregnant. He wanted them to marry, and Pierre wasn't for none of that shit. Five months later the baby got here, a paternity test was done, and it was true what Pierre said. Sarah Romano wasn't as innocent as she claimed to be. Pierre was so mad and said he felt disrespected, so he had to prove a point. He sent Marcus to do his dirty work. Mr. Romano came back to the house accusing Pierre of killing his dogs, and Pierre was all too happy to tell him he wished it was him in the ground instead of his dogs.

Marcell and I walked up to the estate and rang the doorbell. Olivia opened the door smiling like the Cheshire cat. I knew it was all bull-shit when I walked in. I looked around the house, and nothing had changed since I had last been here five years prior. Although elegant, everything was so bland. The entire house was white. We walked to the day room, and Mr. Romano was sitting in there smoking a Cuban cigar. He held his hand towards the other two chairs, and Marcell and I sat down.

"Hello Mr. Romano, you wanted to see me?" He blew smoke out of his mouth before responding.

He looked like death had already grabbed his ass, and all he needed was a grave to fall into. At one point, I respected this man and looked at him like a second father until he started to uphold his daughter's bullshit about leaving Justice. Ever since then I've been looking at his ass sideways. He hasn't reached out to Justice either, but he does send her a nice amount of money monthly. Hell yes, I accept his money; my baby deserves every fucking dime of it.

"Yes, I want to know why you disrespected my daughter by putting your hands on her? She is no longer yours to toy with in such a way. On top of that, you won't let her see my granddaughter because you had some whore at your house." I laughed at him.

"No disrespect to you, but this bitch hasn't seen Justice since she was a day old. Secondly, who I have at my house not your business, Lastly, if she ever decides to try me by disrespecting me again that animal you call a daughter will get trained well." His eyes got big.

"How dare you disrespect me in my house?" This old ass man had some nerve, and if I didn't think he was so close to death, I would have probably put a bullet in his head right then. This conversation was more than over.

"How dare you bring me to your house to disrespect me?" Marcell and I stood up at the same time to leave.

"All these years I thought you were different, but you're just like your brother. You fuck over innocent women." I wanted to beat his old ass for making that statement.

"No, old man. You're delusional as fuck if think anything about those hyenas you raised as daughters are innocent. If you taught them how to act like ladies, you wouldn't have a wore out pussy having and lying ass deadbeat mother for kids. Excuse us; I think it's time we leave." I passed Olivia on the way out.

"You lying bitch." I walked out the door leaving it open.

I swear this bitch tries to find all types of ways to fuck up my life, the only reason I haven't put a bullet in this bitch head is because I thought that one day Justice might want to know her mother. Now her dumb ass wants to start a war because her fucking ego is bruised. This bitch had turned me into a broken man, and I couldn't trust no woman. I've been single for a long time because out of all the shit that I had done for her. She left me like I didn't mean shit. To top that shit off she thought a fucking letter to me justified what she had done. Before I let a muthafucka tear down what my father has built, that bitch will have a diamond encrusted toe tag.

🦋 12 🦋

TAKHIYA

"*Get your ass up you have money to make.*" *My mother kicked my twelve-year-old body hard as hell in the side.*

"*Mom, I just got back in. How can you and dad be out already? I have to sleep. Can I get another hour please?*" *My mother looked at me like I was the scum of the earth.*

"*Bitch, you need to get ready. Eddie is expecting you. Wash your stinking overused ass and leave! My money is waiting, and you know how your daddy gets when he needs his fix. Get the fuck up Khiya and don't let me tell you that again.*" *Yeah, I know how his ass gets; he gets fucking dope sick. I rolled my eyes at my mother and got up.*

My mom walked out the room, and I looked around the room looking for something to put on to meet up with Eddie one of many of my parent's suppliers. Eddie was as mean as they come. I personally felt it was because his dick was about three inches long, and he was the ugliest person I've seen in my life. He was into rough sex. Every time I left I left him, I could barely walk because my body would be bruised and sore from whatever he decided to put in me. I guess I can say the good outweighed the bad when it came to him, because the worst the sex, the more he compensated in drugs.

I looked around for the clothes I had on the previous night. I had a little coke left over. I sat on the filthy mattress poured some coke on my hand and sniffed hard. My nose started running as I felt an instant high and burst of energy. I got up dancing to the beat in my head going to the bathroom when my dad blocked me off at the door.

"You're talking back to your mother?" I couldn't even comment before his hand came across my face knocking me into the wall.

"Dad please, I didn't do anything." I tried to ball up, but he gave me a quick jab to the stomach that made me fall to my knees and fold.

"Now you calling her a liar?" He grabbed me by my hair, pulling me up the wall. He wrapped one of his baseball mitts he calls hands around my neck.

"Don't you ever disrespect my wife like that again, you hear me?" He was waiting on an answer, but I couldn't breathe or nod my head yes. All I could do was let the slob that was coming out of mouth run down his hands.

"Where you want me to put this ungrateful cunt, bae?"

"Drop her ass in the tub, here I come," my mother replied as she walked into the bathroom just in time to see my dad drop me in an empty ass tub. She walked over to the tub and turned the cold water on full blast in my face.

"You'll learn real quick who's running this bitch." She pushed me back down under the water.

I jumped up, screaming at the top of my lungs. I felt a hand come around my waist and me being pulled me to him.

"Bad dream, baby?" I turned, laying back down wrapping my arms around Tyler cuddling close to him.

"Yes!" I stared into the darkness of his room with my head on his chest.

"You want to talk about it?" He rubbed his hands through my thick hair massaging my head relaxing me.

"No!" I shook my head as I was saying it.

That was the truth; I didn't want to talk about it, Tyler was my rebound nigga. Although he was good to me, I didn't see a happily ever after with him. On a good note, he was the total opposite of LaQuan's bum ass. Tyler was goal oriented and wanted more out of life than stunting for the hood. He wasn't a lady's man, most importantly he wasn't gay, and did I mention he was a doctor. Tyler walked up to me at work about a week after the incident with LaQuan. He wanted to know where the smile that he saw every day was. I didn't get into everything that I had gone on with LaQuan, I just told him tomorrow is a better day.

Every day I worked, Tyler would walk his sexy chocolate ass up to me. Standing six feet six inches tall, he would give me the biggest smile I had ever seen. His skin is dark and smooth, and he is built like a god. I almost feel like I need to bow down to him when he walks up to me. Tyler and I have been going strong for about two months now, and he treats me like a queen. Before I could think I want something, he gets it for me. LaQuan and Tyler were like night and day. I felt like I traded in Jordan's for Gucci loafers. The only problem that he can't help me with was the nightmares throughout the night since LaQuan has left.

I held on to Tyler as if my life depended on it and tried to bury the memories of my past. Tyler lifted my face and placed light kisses on my mouth. I kissed him back as he rolled me over on my back. In on swift motion, he was buried deep inside me, slowly rolling his hips taking his time trying to make me forget the dream that had me screaming in the middle of the night. He took my breasts in his mouth and sucked them like he was a baby trying to get full. He took his time building me up until I came on his dick while he kissed my moans away. He laid down still inside of me, when he rolled off me and pulled me into his arms I exhaled a breath still feeling alone and somewhat unsatisfied.

Losing LaQuan has taken pieces of me I didn't know he filled. That nigga was my best friend, and it's going to hard for anyone to replace the emptiness from the hole that man left. I turned on my side thinking about the double I had to do at work tomorrow and forced myself back to sleep.

⚬❧❧

"MERCY HOSPITAL, THIS TAKHIYA, HOW CAN I HELP YOU TODAY?"

I answered the phone at the nurse's station. I listened to the woman's complaint on the end and rolled my eyes placing my hands on my hip. I really didn't feel like it today, so I asked her to hold and transferred her to another floor. As soon as I walked in the door, everything in here went to hell. I came into a code blue and lost one of my patients, the phone hasn't stopped ringing, and two other nurses called off. I put my head in my hands and closed my eyes for about two seconds before I heard Patrice's voice. *Can this shit get any worse?* I thought to myself and walked down to her room picking up her chart.

"Hello Patrice, I'm Takhiya, and I will be your nurse for the rest of my shift. Is there anything I can get you?" I ran the script that I gave every patient that came to my floor. Patrice looked at me, rolling her eyes.

"Yes, you can help me by finding me another nurse." I smiled at her. I really didn't want to help the bitch anyway, but due to our current situation, I had no their choice than to help her. This bitch wasn't going to have me losing my license because she was in her feelings.

"Since we are short of staff today, that would be impossible, but I can call to get you transferred to another floor if that would make you happy." She rolled her eyes at me

"Bitch, anywhere that you are not is perfectly fine with me." I bit down on my lip hard as I could to keep from responding to this hoe.

I gave her a tight smile and walked out the room to put in the transfer. Halfway through her paperwork, I heard screaming coming from her room. What the hell could be going on now, I exhaled loudly and ran into the room to see blood shooting from her IV. I put on my gloves and ran over her.

"No, get your fucking hands off me!" Patrice screamed at me. She just didn't know if this wasn't my livelihood, I would let her ass bleed to death. This bitch has done nothing, but cause me grief my entire life.

"Let me help you. You're bleeding too much." She started pushing me back away from her. If I wasn't at work, I would have let her bleed to death or beat the bitch ass for pushing me. Tyler walked in the room.

"Hello ma'am, I'm Dr. Lay. We need you to calm down and let Nurse Takhiya help you." I tried to grab her hand again, and she pulled away from me.

"Hell no, don't let her touch me she has AIDS. Her nigga was caught with his dick in another man's mouth I know that bitch got something." Before I remembered that I was at work, the words came out my mouth venomously.

"I didn't hear you saying that shit when he had his dick stuck up that black hole you call a pussy in my house."

Tyler's mouth fell open. He was looking at me for an explanation for treating Patrice like the hood rat she was. I wish the bitch would code so that I can shock her ass just to relieve some stress. If you ask me, that ass whipping she got wasn't good enough, especially when the bitch was fucking my man all over my house. Now I have to make sure her ass stay alive. This has to be karma from when I was doing drugs. I didn't say anything else; I just walked out the room, I looked out the window towards the sky.

"Why have thou forsaken me?" I was serious though I needed some answers from the big homie himself.

I got back to my desk and sat down laying my head on the desk.

I heard a man ask "Is Takhiya working today?" I peeped over the desk and saw a man with his back turned to me and a CNA pointing to the desk. I put my head back down and waited for whoever to walk over to me.

"Takhiya?" the man asked questioningly.

"Yes, it's me!" I responded without raising my head up the man laughed.

"Bad day, huh?" he asked while laughing.

"If you only knew." I lifted my head off the desk.

"Bryce!"

৩৫৩

I GOT INTO MY TRUCK AND PULLED OFF. MY THREE-DAY SUSPENSION will give me some time to reflect on some things. I really think that Tyler's time with me has passed. It's not because of the suspension; it's because as soon as this trick opened her mouth about me, he hung on to every word she said, without even thinking about it. I turned on my radio and didn't know what the hell I was listening too. I was getting ready to stop the CD when I heard the "Poppa Was A Rolling Stone" beat drop.

I never had a loving mother. She abandons my love blame for her struggle budgets and uncover. Call me bitches and motherfuckas. As I got older, I disrespected her and never came home for supper. Outside fighting getting tougher sold two for fifteen ninth grade making snow buffer. Break in your house I'm taking everything before I leave my signature move is turning on your oven. Waiting to see your death on the news or waiting for mine because I have I have nothing to lose, fourteen years old heart already bruised. Trying to be grown man because but I ain't got a clue for real. Daddy did seventeen in the pen he's the reason why I'm mean with the pen a boy without a father grew very hurt. Mama fucking niggas every day they coming out of there. First day of school holes in my shoes no new clothes no girl want to be my boo. Everybody laughing at me like a got damn fool. I grew up insecure well I still am too mama said she wish she had an abortion. My reply you should've stop pushing, I was forced in. If it were up to me, I would've stayed where the Lord knows I wasn't ready for courses. I was a kid when you beat me till my nose bleed. I pray to God I would wake and your ass dead, you love me like you love them niggas in the feds.

My mouth dropped. Whoever this was on this song was saying everything I felt about I bout my parents. It was like he had a personal window to my soul, I pulled the CD out to see who was the nigga that was spitting so much real shit. "Wisqo" I never heard of him, but I hope he makes it.

I pulled up to my house and got out the car thinking about Bryce, and what would I wear on our dinner date. I had to redirect my thoughts because this damn Wisqo had me all in my feelings.

13

MARCELL

"I have a delivery for, Bailey Turner." After a couple of minutes passed, I heard the locks on the door turn and the door open. I dropped the box to the ground to see Bailey pointing a gun in my face.

"Damn I see you not happy to see me." Bailey laughed and turned around leaving the door the open for me.

"Nigga, I wasn't expecting any packages, and most of the time they are left at the front desk. Living in Chiraq anything can happen, and you won't catch me slipping." She sat the gun on the table, and I walked behind her, and it picked up.

"You have nice taste." I took the clip out and popped the bullet out of the chamber sitting the baby nine down and putting my two nines next to hers. She looked at me like I was crazy and went and sat the couch folding her legs under her.

Bailey and I had started fucking around the day after Bryce was shot, her fierce ass attitude and smart mouth had a nigga ready from when she took up for Takhiya. I usually don't like my women so damn rowdy and outspoken, but when she slapped me that shit turned me own. I wanted nothing more than to hog tie her little ass and give her the dick until she tapped out.

"Why do I have to take this bitch anywhere? I know y'all saw her slap the shit out of me yesterday and today all is supposed to be forgiven. Get the fuck out of here with that. Another thing didn't nobody start taking shots at us until these bitches came from Chicago. None of y'all think this shit is suspect, and now you want me to go out and get shot too. Just put me a bed big bro I bet I come back here stretched out." I looked at Pierre and Marcus. I was dead serious, and all they were doing was laughing at me like shit was joke.

"I know you're not scared of Bailey's lil' ass; she wouldn't hurt a fly. But really, how did you expect her to act when you were being disrespectful as fuck to them? They don't know who we are and how much power comes behind the Mariano name. To them, you're just some random disrespectful, rude ass nigga. You can't get mad because they demand respect. Nigga, you're going to have to learn to deal with the shit, because I plan on making her my baby mama."

Marcus looked at me with a slick grin on his face. What he didn't know is that Bailey would run circles around his ass. I turned and walked towards the door.

"Bring your ass on, man." Bailey looked at the wall then back at me then at the wall again.

"Who in the hell are you talking to?" She turned to the wall.

"He must be talking to you because I know for a fact his retarded ass ain't coming at me like that." Pierre busted out laughing

"You two have fun and don't kill each other while y'all out."

Bailey got up and came to the door. I slammed it in her face before she could grab the doorknob. I started laughing and walked to the car. When she got in the car, she was livid. I laughed as I drove to the hotel. The tension in the car was thick. Fuck not cutting it with a knife; you couldn't saw through that shit. We pulled up to the hotel, and Bailey jumped out the truck fast, bent down, then casually walked into the hotel. I sat in the car for about forty minutes when one of the bellmen walked to the car.

"Excuse me sir, but your tires on the passenger side is flat."

I got out the car, and I was pissed. I texted Marcus for her room number and walked right to the elevator. When I stepped out on the fourth floor, Bailey was in the hall with her back to me talking to some guy with a glass in her hand. She had changed into a pair of shorts, and a tank top, and her ass was looking fat as hell. I walked up behind her wrapping my hand around her waist tightly.

"Walk away, man." The guy walked to the elevator without looking back. I open the door to the room, pushing Bailey in while she laughed at me.

"I see you got the present I left you." She really thought this shit was funny. I took the glass she had in her hand and threw it across the room. She didn't even blink at me; she just burst out in laughter. I pushed her on the bed.

"You think shit is funny, huh? I swear I can't stand a smart mouth ass bitch." She reached up and double smacked my ass.

"You don't know what your mother was before she had you, and this needs to be the last time you address me as anything other than my fucking name Marcell, or I will gut your ass like a fish I swear."

I felt something poke me a little bit, I looked down at her hand, and she was holding a fucking knife to my navel. I swear motherfuckas wasn't lying when they said that Chicago women are in a fucking class of their own. I snatched the knife from her, took the sheet off the bed, and tied her hands up. Her lil' ass was crazy as hell.

After I tied her up, she wrapped her legs around me pulling me to her and kissed me. I took the knife she had just pulled on me and cut her clothes off her. I stood back and looked at her body. Bailey ass was stacked. Her brown skin was smooth and silky, her pussy was waxed, and when she opened her legs, her shit was glistening. I didn't even take off my clothes before I bent down to taste her. As soon as my tongue touched her, she started moaning and rolling her hips on me.

I knew I had to bring my A game with her smart mouth ass. I put licked her whole pussy then put my face all in her shit. I stoke my tongue in her, did my tornado move, and went back to her clit. I stuck two of my fingers up in her, and when she locked her legs around my head, her entire body vibrated. She screamed my name loud as she squirted in my mouth; I stood up with her juices all over my face and started taking my clothes off. She got on her knees in front of me and took my dick in her mouth without blinking. My knees buckled; this bitch had mad skills. I started fucking her mouth, and she was taking all that shit.

I pulled away from her, putting a condom on and rammed right into her. She tried to back away from me.

"Naw ma, you talked all that smart mouth shit; take this dick."

I pulled her closer to me, and she put her hands on my stomach to get me from going deeper than I was. I took the end of the sheet and tied it to the head-

board. I came back to her and slammed into her again. She was moaning loud. Once she adjusted to my size, she started working her muscles on me. I saw then that she just had to have shit her way. I'm not gone lie she was working my ass over, and I was at my breaking point. I pulled back then went back into her, when she locked her legs around me and released them.

"Let that shit go ma, come for me. Show daddy he's put in good work. Come for me bae, let go." Bailey locked her legs on me.

"MARCELL!!!" She soaked my stomach squirting.

"Yeah baby, that's right."

"So, where's my box?" I walked back to the door, getting the box and placed it in front of her.

"What is it?" she picked it up.

"Just open it, damn. Do you have to question everything?" She pulled a knife from her bra, and I smiled. This fucking girl doesn't trust nobody. She opened the box and threw it at my head. I blocked it and started laughing.

"After not seeing me for three months this is what the fuck you bring me, just a box?" She pouted at me.

"Naw bae, I brought you some pipe. You know I have the Midas touch with this motherfucka." I grabbed my dick, and she started laughing.

"Nope nigga, Midas is your tongue because when you touched me with that, I swear I saw everything in gold for weeks." I looked her up and down.

"Yeah well let daddy touch you now."

I walked over to her and laid her back. I pushed her panties to the side and stuck my tongue in her pussy. I used my finger to play with her clit. When I replaced my finger with my tongue, she started moaning, lifted her hips, and pushed my head deeper into her. I ate her pussy until she started vibrating on my tongue. I ripped her panties off and pulled my pants down. I picked her up putting my dick in her and pushed her against the wall. She wrapped her legs around me, and I fucked her hard.

"You like the present daddy got for you?" She wrapped her arms tight around me but didn't say anything. I dropped down and put her back on the floor.

"Oh you can't talk, right?" I pushed her legs to her ears and slammed into her.

"Ahh!" I pulled out and just gave her the tip then slammed into her. I kept that routine up until she answered.

"Yes, daddy I love your gift!" She cried out while she came again.

I helped her up and went to the room. She sat on the bed and before I could stop her she popped my dick in her mouth. She worked me over with her mouth I felt the buildup and knew I was at my breaking point and looked down at her.

"Swallow." She caught all my children and gave them a warm place to stay. If this girl didn't watch out, she could be wifey.

Most bitches let me run circles around their ass, but not Bailey. She listens when she wants to and the only time that was is in the bedroom. She didn't take my shit and would check me in a heartbeat. After she and Takhiya left Miami, we kept in touch. We would talk every day once she got off work. One time I didn't answer the phone for her and called her back at two o'clock in the morning.

"What are doing?"

"I'm sleep nigga; you should have answered when I called you, but instead you were out fucking some bitch and couldn't answer because she probably had your dick in her mouth at the time. Get off my line nigga; I have to work in the morning, unlike that bitch you were with." She hung up the phone.

I stood my dumb ass there looking at the screen saver on my phone because I couldn't believe she did that. Did I mention she was right about the entire situation? Bailey wouldn't answer my calls for two weeks.

We laid down in the bed and just chilled. I looked at her.

"What happened with that little problem you and Takhiya had with that nigga?" Bailey had told me what went down when they got back to Chicago.

"We still haven't seen that nigga, and if he's smart he'd be hiding up and eagle's ass praying he doesn't shit. To this day Takhiya still wants to beat his ass."

I laughed at her little saying, but I knew it was more to this shit then she was telling me.

"Why did you open the door with a gun in my face Bailey, and why do you have a knife in your bra? Don't come with that I live in Chicago shit because you should feel safe in your home." She put her head in my chest then looked up at me.

"We haven't seen Quan, but he did put a price on my head. No one has come for me so far, but that shit can change once the right mother-fucka needs that cash." I nodded my head understanding where she was coming from. She'd rather be safe than sorry.

"My brothers and me are going to be out here for a while taking care of business, I have to go right now, but if you need me call me."

I got up to put on my clothes and walked to the bedroom door. She's taken care of herself for these couple of months and could last for a couple more hours, but before I leave to go back to Miami, I'm going to make sure this shit is taken care of.

"Aye, if your nigga ain't going to be here tonight can I come back?" She threw a pillow at me, and I laughed.

"Get the spare key out of the drawer in the kitchen closest to the door." I nodded at her and walked out the door.

❧ 14 ❧

BRYCE

I pulled back up to the hotel with a big ass smile on my face. Seeing Takhiya had made day until Pierre got in the car, and I could tell he was in a fucked up mood, which seemed to be a lot lately. It was like he and Marcell had switched personalities. Marcell was happy, joking all the time and this nigga was mad at the world. I felt like I should be the one pissed off hell, my big brother had let me down. His job was to keep us safe, and this nigga couldn't even pinpoint who tried to kill me.

The video of the shooting had been erased, and no one knew a thing. The streets weren't even talking, so whoever did it moved silently as hell. I was trying to just get over the shit, I'm still here, and that should be all that matters. Pierre was deep in feelings though.

Everyone in Miami knew that the one thing you didn't do was come for the Mariano boys because we didn't play about our shit. If you came for us, we came back harder, and when we did, no one was safe. Pierre had no mercy. He would kill your mother and kids then sit and have dinner right after. I thought back to what Olivia said after I smacked her and the meeting with her father that went left.

"P you think Olivia followed through with her threat the night of the grand opening?" He looked at me like I was crazy.

I didn't think the shit I was asking was too farfetched, Mr. Romano never liked Pierre and I know I'm on his shit as of recently. Plus, he felt like we had done his daughters wrong and disrespected him. There have been plenty of wars over pussy since the beginning of time it didn't matter whose pussy it was. Wives pussy, daughter's pussy, mother's pussy, sister's pussy, cousin's pussy, and even boy's pussy.

"I'm saying it's not like she couldn't have pulled it off. She has the money, and her dad would back her." He thought about it.

"I mean it's not impossible, but if her dad didn't kill you after she left, I don't think he would try now knowing that Olivia doesn't give a damn about Justice."

He made a valid point her old man was sick and didn't have much time left. If he did kill me, Justice would be in the world alone fucking with the bitch that birthed her. Olivia's father knew that Justice best chance at a normal life was with me.

"I told you the day you met Olivia not to fuck with her, I knew she was nutty as squirrel shit, but no you were in love." He was right about that too, but I thought he only said that because of the shit with him and Sarah. How the fuck was I supposed to both sisters was fucked up in the head?

"How long do we have before we get to Natalie's house?" I kept my eyes on the road while and switched lanes, Chicago traffic was the devil and people were so fucking rude that I wanted to shoot out their tires. I looked at the GPS.

"It says forty minutes, but it could be longer in this traffic." I glanced at him and had mean mug back on his face. This guy had cut me off and was talking shit.

"Get on the side of this fool."

I switched lanes lining up with the car that cut me off, and the guy flipped us the bird. Pierre let his window down and pointed his thirty-eight at the guy causing him to run off the road. I laughed so hard that man looked like he shitted on his self, Pierre mugged the shit out of me.

"P, what's going on with you bro?" His face changed to a worse look.

"Nigga you're already the ugly brother, please don't make it worst."
He frowned at me even more.

"How dare you talk about my ailment?" I laughed at him my
parents didn't make ugly kids, but we all looked better than Pierre
no homo.

Pierre put a sneaky smile on his face and started messing with the
radio the music blasted.

Promises you made me, all the things you told me
You said you'd never leave me
We'll be together for eternity.
Now it's all in the past.
Now I know our love will last.
Lady, I will do all I can.
Lady, I will be all I am.
I'll give you all you've had before.
So, come on in and close the door.
Let me show you what I could be.
Could you just please tell me, will you believe in love
and the promise that it gives?

HE KNEW I HATED THAT SONG OLIVIA AND I DANCED TO THAT AT
our wedding I mean mugged him.

"Low blow." I turned the radio off, and we rode the last twenty
minutes in silence.

The day I married Olivia was the best day of my life, she came down the
aisle in an all-white. She had red roses for her bouquet, and a fully bloomed red
rose in hair with rhinestones on her curls that was looped into a bun. Her veil
covered her beautiful face, and I swore I was the happiest man on earth. I prac-
tically raped her mouth in the church when we said I do. The priest cleared his
throat several times before we stopped kissing.

On the ride to the reception in the limo, I had to take my wife down. I
hadn't seen her in twenty-four hours. That was the longest we hadn't been
together and missed being inside of her. motherfuckas wasn't lying when they
said pregnant pussy was the best pussy. Olivia would be so wet that I thought
her water bag was leaking. We walked into our reception twenty minutes late

and "Love You For Life" by Jodeci played on cue." That was truly the best night of my life with the woman I loved so much that I would have given her my last breath.

I never thought that Olivia and I would be at the point that we're at now. She still loves me, but I swear I hate her. She took what I gave her so freely my love and my seed and said fuck us. She's the type of baby mama that makes you want to reach in her ass and take your nut back.

We pulled up to Natalie's house, and before we could ring the bell, the door flung open, and she was speaking Italian. I could tell she was pissed. Once she saw us standing in front of her, a big smile spread across her face.

"Hey, cousin." Natalie hugged both Pierre and me with a smile on her face.

"What are you doing here Bryce? You should be somewhere healing." She looked at me and hugged me again.

"I'm fine and laying down is the last thing I want to do. I just wanted to let you know we are going to be in Chicago for a while on business and to see how you're doing." She looked at the both of us.

"It's just the two of you?" As soon as the words left her mouth, Marcell and Marcus pulled up.

"So, what kind of business has you all coming from the sunshine state?" She raised her eyebrow at us.

"Bitches," Pierre stated with so much disdain that we all looked at him and Marcell stepped up to him.

"The only bitch I see around here is you. You've been on your period since Bryce got shot. We were all scared for him, but the only person you should be pissed at is yourself for letting the shit happen."

Shit was getting real, and I knew they were about to fight because every time we check Pierre, he wants to try to remind us he's the oldest. I was going to sit back and watch who would come out on top.

"Bet twenty grand Marcell beats Pierre ass." I leaned over telling Marcus. He smiled.

"I'll take your money. Pierre's had been in rare form lately. Sorry to tell you, but he's finna beat the hell out Marcell." Marcus pulled out his phone.

"I'm recording this shit. Just in case you do win, I need to make my money back. World Star!!!!" Marcus yelled, and we both laughed.

Natalie stepped between them.

"Save your energy and come help me handle some business." We all looked at each other and as she walked to my car and got in the front seat. We got in our cars and pulled off.

We pulled up to a building, and we got out of the car. Natalie walked into the building with us close behind her.

"Hey, Jason," Natalie said with a smile on her face, Jason turned to her smiling and her before he could say anything Natalie pulled a big ass nine from her purse.

POW! The shot echoed through the building. She turned to us.

"You know how this shit goes no witnesses."

Pierre had his gun out already. This was the first time in months I saw any resemblance of being happy on his face.

🎇 15 🎇

PATRICE

I laid in the hospital bed content with the fact that I had gotten Takhiya in trouble; I hope she gets fired and loses that fine ass doctor. I could tell he liked her ass. When he walked in the room, he was more worried about what was going on with her than with me. He looked at her like she was the only woman in the world, I would kill to have any man look at me like that, and this bitch got the nerve to have two niggas all over her.

I don't care what's going I just can't stand to see that bitch happy. The doctor walked back in the room after speaking with Takhiya.

"I apologize for the way my nurse spoke to you earlier. Know that she has been reprimanded and it won't happen again." I stared at him.

"Don't mind that ratchet bitch you can take that drugged out hoe out the hood, but you can't make they ass act civilized." I leaned back in my bed letting that shit sink in with him. Anytime I feel that anything is going good with her, I'm trying to destroy that shit.

"What do you mean drugged out hoe?" I looked at him like I was shocked that she hadn't told him about her past, but doctor or not niggas always fall for pussy. This man didn't know me from a can of paint and was finna fall for everything I'm telling. This nigga a whole goofy, but I like them like that they're so gullible.

"I don't know maybe I shouldn't say anything it's not my business that you're fucking a bitch that used to sell pussy for her next high. I feel like that shit is between y'all, but you might want to get checked out before you raw dog the next bitch." His mouth dropped opened and his eyes got big.

"I'm sorry what did you say?" I thought to myself *bingo*!

"I'm just saying, you can question me on it if you want to, but Takhiya and I have been in school together since Pre-K. I may not know all of the details behind the shit that she did, but I do know that she was less than your common thot. That girl has had a drug habit since sixth grade and has been selling pussy even longer. On top of all that, her boyfriend of many years was recently caught getting his dick sucked by his best friend and right-hand man. So, while you're in here trying to save your lover, you might need to be getting checked out." I was getting happier than a sissy with a bag of dicks just looking at his expression. This bitch life was over; it was just time to put the icing on the cake.

"What do you mean right-hand man?" This shit was so easy. This nigga falls right into my trap each time. What kills me is men swear woman be ready for the juice, but niggas drink from the cup just as easily.

"You don't know that your girl is big time drug dealer? Her ex-boyfriend, his best friend, along with her best friend Bailey is as big as they come on the west side of Chicago. They supply everybody." This nigga didn't ask any more questions. He just walked out of the room, and that's what you call a grand finale.

I set back on my bed grabbed my iPad and starting reading *Love and War: A Hoover Gang Affair 2"* by Latoya Nicole. That bitch knew her pen game was tight as hell. It was just getting good when I heard a voice that I just knew I wouldn't hear again.

"You hear me talking to you. I said what's up?"

I damn near pissed on myself because I didn't know if this nigga was still mad at me for taking his truck or not. I know he thinks I'm the one that dropped the engine in it too, but that wasn't my doing. I started shaking. Hell, I was in the best place for him to fuck me; I'm sure if he beats my ass the nurses would come and clean my ass up.

"Hey Quan." He started smiling, but I didn't see shit funny my voice was quivering and shit.

"Damn, are you cold? You need me to get somebody to turn the air down for you or something?" He knew damn well I wasn't cold. He smiled, and his eyes looked sneaky as hell as he closed the door to the room. I started looking around for something to beat his ass with, and I grabbed the pole my IV was connected too.

"Look, Quan, you see I'm down. I'm not trying to fight you about some shit that happened months ago. Let that shit go, nigga." He walked over to the bed.

"I'm not on shit, Patrice. I just came to see how you were doing. I stopped by your house, and your mom said you were rushed to the hospital." I was still looking at his ass like he had two heads this nigga needed something.

"I'm straight man I just have pancreatitis, nothing major."

He nodded his head at me and rubbed my titties. He moved his hand down and stuck one of his fingers in me, then pulled out and put them him his mouth. My pussy instantly started pulsating. I don't give a fuck what's hurting on me when it comes to dick a bitch be ready like the Cowboys during football season. However, for a minute I forgot who had their hand in my shit. I closed my legs up on his hand, and he pulled his fingers out of me.

"Hold on nigga' they just caught you with your whole dick in Jason's mouth." His eyes hit the floor for a minute.

"Bitch, I'm not gay. As bad as this shit sounds, that nigga drugged and took advantage of me." I laughed at him.

"It looked like you enjoyed it to me." Quan looked like he wanted to beat my ass, but he just stared me down.

"That's the same shit Takhiya said when I tried to explain myself to her." He looked so sad, so when he said, that my heart melted.

"I'll listen to you, babe. Whatever it is you know I got you, right?" Quan pulled me to him kissed me.

"I need somewhere to hide out for a little while. Do you think you can help me with that?" I knew if I played my part long enough I would eventually get what I wanted. This is my time to prove I could be that down ass bitch he needed. I had been telling y'all all along that

Takhiya wasn't that bitch. There's no way in hell you can turn a real hoe into a housewife. The only thing she was good for was doing dicks.

"You know I got you, baby."

Quan pushed my gown up opened my legs and made love to my pussy with his mouth. This nigga had never gone in on me like that before; he had me coming back to back. When he got up, he pulled his pants down. He smelled a little sweaty, and his balls were little musty, but I wasn't going to turn him down. He must have known he wasn't that fresh because when I grabbed his dick to suck it, he pushed my head back and climbed in the bed with me. I opened up my legs for him. Once he entered me, he rolled all in my pussy.

His dick was so big that while he fucked me, I could the imprint of his shit in my stomach. This nigga was doing shit he had never done to my pussy, and he had me squirting all over the bed. I kind of felt bad for the motherfucka that's had to come clean up after this. For real, though I now know why Takhiya's ass was going crazy and beating my ass over this dick. This nigga could lay shit down. After having me come so many times, I lost count, and he busted a nut. He cleaned himself up, and I handed him the keys to my house. He wasn't gone ten minutes before I was in a deep ass sleep.

16

LAQUAN

I knew if no one else would help me Patrice would. That thot has loved me for years. You would think as much as I have looked over her ass that she'd have lost all interest in me. Hell after the last time Khiya beat her ass; she should have second thoughts about anything that has to do with me. That bitch thinks she's slick. I heard everything she told that doctor about Takhiya and me. On me, she not getting away with all that gay shit she was talking about me. She figures she has what she wants, but she could never be half the woman Takhiya is. She played on homeboy feelings, and I played on hers. I bet she didn't think karma was coming to her ass that soon. On some real shit though, I have more important shit to think about than that bitch.

I rolled my blunt, and then pulled out of the hospital parking lot before I blazed up. I really had a lot of shit on my mind that I had to figure out before a motherfucka caught me slipping. Usually, I would sit back and talk to Jason about things I had on my mind, but since that nigga raped me and is now dead, so it ain't shit he could tell me. I was planning on killing his ass anyway, but motherfuckas beat me to it. Jason had been fucking up anyway. This nigga had caused some bad blood between my connect and me some months ago. They gave us a couple of weeks to come up with the money that he fucked up, which was gracious for them mob niggas.

When Jason and I first started fucking with these Florida niggas, we were making money hand over fucking fist. We were making the trip out of town at least three times a week that the niggas started fronting us half of what we bought. Once we started taking over half the west side, I guess Jason wanted to see what was making these crack and coke addicts go crazy over our shit. That nigga started using, but since he was my nigga, I tried to overlook shit as long as he wasn't cutting into my money and the money we owe out.

About two weeks before Takhiya went to Miami, little by little more drugs came up missing. When we didn't have the money to re-up, I asked Khiya for it, but after the shit with Patrice, Takhiya left my ass hanging. What makes matters worse is that Jason found some bitch that was dropping mad weight in the burbs, so he started grabbing drugs from her to compensate what he fucked up. We all know that shit didn't go so well, this nigga fucked up with her too. She put the word out that she was coming for our ass, and I didn't have shit to do with the deal. I'm just guilty by association on this shit.

I hadn't seen Jason since the night he was on bullshit. I had been looking everywhere for his ass, but I knew he would go back to the trap soon. I was out bending block and saw that nigga in traffic. I knew I probably wouldn't get the chance to get at his ass if I didn't follow him then. He went to the trap, and since I hadn't been around like that, I didn't know who he had been working with. I didn't want to walk into no bullshit because I was in feelings about how shit went down with him. I drove around the back and looked in the windows; it was about ten niggas in there that I didn't know.

I was getting ready to come to the back door shooting everybody until one of their ass took me out when a bitch came warehouse said something and shot Jason in the head. It was four niggas with her that started taking them niggas down quick. One of the niggas looked like he found pleasure in killing they ass. Once they killed everyone in the room, they bagged up the rest of the product and the money. I needed all of the product and money they took. After that, I knew I didn't have a chance in the world to stay by myself.

I was out here bad as hell, and the word that was going around is the bitch that was looking for us name was Natalie, and she had ties to the mob. It wasn't really shit I could do about any of this. I had two different organizations of the mob looking for me. One of their asses would eventually succeed in taking me out, but before I go, I'm taking that bitch Bailey with me. That's what I really needed Patrice for, that bitch always knew how to find Takhiya and Bailey even when I couldn't. Patrice is a petty, jealous bitch, but if I had to sell this bitch dreams of forever to get what I need, then that's what I have to do. What Patrice didn't know is that forever wouldn't be that long for me, I'm a dead man walking, and I know it.

Even though I had unfinished business with Bailey, I needed to get to my baby Takhiya too. I had to tell her the truth behind all this and the fact that I probably put her in a dangerous situation was fucking with me. I wanted to talk to her at the hospital, but all that shit Patrice was talking had fucked me up. To know that Takhiya's messing with that fuck boy doctor had fucked me up too. I know I had fucked up with her, but she wasn't supposed to move on that quick.

Karma was kicking me in my ass. All the shit I had done to Khiya, I was getting back triple, and after that, death would be at the door.

❧ 17 ❧

TYLER

I know we are basically fuck buddies, but I love the shit out of Takhiya. She's my dream girl. She has dinner waiting on me every time I go over her house. She washes my clothes when I work twenty hours out the day, and since I've been taking her to different functions, she's kept all my events in order and is the perfect hostess when I have parties. Her head and pussy game is unexplainable. The first time I fucked her, I should have planted my seed in her. The only one thing she needs to work on is her weight, and I've been introducing her to the gym slowly. I treat her like the queen she deserves to be treated like and try to do everything I can to keep that lame ass dude she was messing with out of her head.

After talking with the Patrice today, I found a lot of shit about her that I would have never expected from her. All that shit I can forgive, but stepping out on me with some random ass nigga I can't. I already know I'm kind of pussy whipped because she's taking me out of my character. I don't give a damn about being a pussy whipped man; they have the best marriages because they love their wives more than anything.

I sat in my car in front of the restaurant looking at my girl with this nigga that popped up at the hospital the other day. She sat across from him smiling looking like she was mesmerized by him. I couldn't believe this shit. After fucking with her for three months, she still treated me like I was a piece of fucking meat. Most of her calls or text to me was about her about busting a nut. I mean we went on dates and shit, but I can tell that I was just a man with a dick to her. I had asked her about her past just trying to get her to open up to me, but she was so vague with me I just it slide.

Honestly, I didn't give a fuck about her past. It takes a strong woman to overcome the shit Patrice had told me about her. That was the type of woman I needed by my side. It takes a lot to deal with the type of man I am. As I watched the interactions between them, I felt myself getting more pissed that this man could come out of nowhere and just capture Takhiya's attention like this.

It was like she hung on to every word he said. I wonder if she's doing this punish me for suspending her. I could have simply ignored the shit Patrice told me; it's not like she tried to make things easier for her. Patrice antagonized her until Takhiya lashed out at her. I could tell that Patrice didn't mean anyone that was involved with Takhiya any good. It was like Patrice wanted to ruin her in any way she could.

Later that night I stopped by Takhiya's house, and she told me about how Patrice had sex with her boyfriend in her house. If you asked me Takhiya handled herself very well compared to what I would have done being in that situation.

I looked back into the window, and Takhiya's lips were locked to this nigga. I gripped the steering wheel tighter. I really couldn't wrap my mind around this shit. This nigga didn't even have enough class to pick her up from home; she drove herself to the restaurant. My phone alerted me that her car was in motion. I knew it was going to be some shit as soon as it went off, and she was going in the opposite direction of Bailey's house. I grabbed my phone to look at the cameras I had installed in her car and saw she had on a cocktail dress.

I gave her about thirty minutes before I walked out of my house and I tracked her car here. It was one thing to go out on this date, but to act like she doesn't have a man in her life is fucked up, and in general, it was fucking me up. She leaned in and kissed him again, and I lost. I know all of you think I'm crazy, but I'm far from that. I'm just territorial. I got out of my car walking into the prestigious restaurant to be stopped at the door by one of the hostess.

"Hello sir, how can I help you this evening?" I tried to walk past her, and she stepped in front of me.

"You can help me by getting the fuck out of my way."

Every move I made this bitch was blocking me, and I was getting tired of her bullshit. She sidestepped me one too many time, and I tripped her ass. I walked right in the restaurant, as she tried to get up in the four-inch heels she had on. When I laid my eyes on Takhiya, she was holding this nigga's hand. I walked towards the table pulling a chair from one of the tables across from them, and the lady sitting at the table started to say something.

"Shut up bitch; I'm not trying to hear the shit." Her mouth dropped open, and she put her hand on her chest.

"Well, I've never." I gave her a menacing look.

"And you never will with the way you look." Takhiya was so busy with her lover boy that she didn't even hear the transaction.

I slid the chair to their table and sat down quickly. Takhiya turned with a shocked expression on her face. She frowned but didn't say anything. Her date sat there looking amused.

"What's wrong Takhiya, his dick got your tongue?" She squinted her eyes at me.

"What are you doing here Tyler, and what's with the disrespectful shit?" I looked between Takhiya and her boy toy.

"I think the question should be what is my girlfriend doing out with another man? You're in here kissing all over him like I don't even fucking exist." Takhiya raised her eyebrow at me.

"Girlfriend? We never agreed to that shit. We are not in a *relationship*." She put emphases on relationship like the word disgusted her when referring to herself and me.

"I'm a grown woman and free to kiss or fuck who I please. I see you're not yourself at the moment, I think you need to leave."

"Oh, you think I need to leave? While you're thinking let me tell you what the fuck I know. I know that when I leave this motherfucker, you're coming with me. You can either walk out of here with me or get carried; the choice is yours." Takhiya's date hadn't said anything the entire time.

"Tyler, whatever you thought we had is over; please leave." I laughed at her ass right before I grabbed her ass by that thick ass bun on her head. Her date jumped out of his chair, knocking it to the floor while grabbing my arm.

"It's time for you to leave, nigga." I let go of Takhiya's hair and picked up the champagne bottle that was on the table raising it up to crack his ass with it. The guy took his free hand and cracked me over the head with a gun. The champagne bottle I had in my hand crashed on the floor as I stumbled backwards.

"It's a lot of shit I deal with, but a motherfucka being disrespectful isn't one of them. You need to leave now and know that the only reason you ain't dead is because it's too many witnesses in here." The guy still had his gun on me. I wanted to rush ass, but I valued my life.

"You're going to pay for this shit. You don't know who I am. You don't know the people that I'm very acquainted with and what I can do to you," I told him in a lethal tone. His ass didn't get the memo, but he would soon.

He gave me the same look that I gave him.

"Honestly, I don't give a fuck who you are or who you know; say less, nigga." He sat down but kept his gun on me. I looked at him than Takhiya.

"This shit ain't over."

I turned and walked out. When I got to my car, the police were walking in the restaurant. Takhiya may have gotten away with this shit, but it was far from over. I pulled off and went straight to her house. When she got home, it was after one o'clock. As soon as she walked in the house, I pulled out my phone to watch the cameras I had in her house.

❧ 18 ❧

TAKHIYA

I can't believe the shit that Tyler pulled tonight. I should have known that his ass was crazy, after our second date when he told me he was falling in love. He would get all possessive, pulling me close to him to him even when we were around Bailey. At first, I thought it was cute until he started questioning everywhere I went. If I didn't tell him, he would always he ride pass somewhere and see me. Now that I think about it, he has always shown me signs of him being crazy than a motherfucka. Even though he tried to ruin my night, Bryce made the best of it.

I walked into my house and began stripping at the door. Just the thought of Bryce had my pussy soaking wet. I walked up the stairs pulling out some shorts and a tank top to sleep in. I then grabbed my vibrator and went straight to the shower. I adjusted the dial on the showerhead to pulse and stepped in closing the glass door behind me. I thought about the night that I had with Bryce.

"Takhiya, I'm not trying to get into your personal life, but you need to let buddy go." I sat at the table embarrassed by the scene that Tyler had caused.

"I'm sorry that this happened, Bryce. The night was going so perfect too." Bryce grabbed my hand.

"The night is still perfect, ma. I'm just saying though. You see I tried to just

sit back and let you handle your business, but the shit that nigga did was disrespectful. I'm not the type of nigga that lets shit like that go. You have to understand Takhiya; I'm not your average nigga on the streets. The type lifestyle you're used to from fucking with your ex-boyfriend is not the type of lifestyle that I lead. To make shit clearer for you, I'm more like the connects connect. The reason I'm telling you this is because I see a much better life for you. Ma, you need to be a kept woman. You work so hard trying to maintain a decent lifestyle when I can give you a better one. Let me keep you, ma. You saved a nigga life when you could have easily walked away. A lot of women ain't cut out for what I do, but I know you are in a class of your own."

I sat there and listened to everything he said, but I wasn't going to just agree to some shit. Didn't he see what just happened with that crazy ass Tyler? I guess he noticed the questioning look on my face.

"Ma, you have been upholding the wrong nigga all this time. Just think of the moves you can make and how far you can get by fucking with the right nigga."

He made so much sense Quan had saved my life as a child, but when it came to shit that I needed as a woman, he wasn't good for shit. On top of that, all that gay shit just killed my soul.

"If I agree to this, what do you want from me?" Bryce looked at me.

"All I want is honesty and loyalty. I'm not going to sugar coat this shit for you committing to me is basically giving your life away. You already know that in Miami I'm a very powerful man and my reach is beyond what you think, baby. It will be shit that you will see and some shit that you may have to do that you won't agree with." I took what he was saying in and but I had to cut him off.

"Bryce, it's a lot of shit that you don't know about me, but the real question I want to ask is why me?" He gave me a serious expression.

"Why not you, ma? Do you think you're unworthy of being with a mob boss?" My mouth dropped.

"A mob what?" I raised my voice a little; he had to be fucking kidding. Did people in the mob just announce they shit like that?

"Come on let's go." Bryce paid the bill and pulled my chair out for me to get up. When we walked out the door, there was a horse and carriage on the streets. He pulled me close to him, walking me towards the carriage. I started smiling.

"This is for us?" He nodded his head, and we sat silent for a few minutes before he started to speak again.

"Khiya, I know what I want, and I know that you would be perfect for me. Any woman that's willing to put her own life on the line for me is more than worthy of sitting beside me." I took in what he said not sure if this was something I wanted to embark in.

"Bryce, when I was younger my parents sold me to their drug dealers for money. I was repeatedly raped and fed drugs. By the time I was a teenager, I was an addict and somewhat of a prostitute. I appreciate all that you see in me, but with the past that I have, I don't see anything good coming from us being in a relationship. Bryce looked at me like I had lost my mind.

"Takhiya, your past is just that, a past. I know what I want, and from experience, you know I get what I want." I crossed my legs because every time he bossed up on me, it made me horny as hell.

"Just let me think about it ok."

"I'll give you that, but don't make me wait too long."

Bryce was sitting here acting like this shit was simple as hell. I know what the hell Quan had to do just to put the streets on lock. Sometimes I had to be his wingman and fuck with a couple of the heavys in the street so that he could come in and do what he does. Fucking with someone in the mob was an entirely different level of shit.

"Yes Bryce, make this pussy come baby!"

My vibrator was doing its job, but it wasn't as good as having Bryce right here with me. I pinched my nipples as I moved the vibrator faster in a circular motion. Once I felt the need to pee, I pushed and squirted across the shower. I stuck my finger in pussy to keep the feeling going as long as possible.

"Yes baby, you always make this pussy come like that." I laid on the shower floor for a minute until my body got over the feeling of euphoria.

I opened my eyes getting off the shower floor when the glass to the shower came crashing down on me. I held my head down and saw the water mixing with my blood washing it down the drain.

"Bitch, you in here wishing this nigga was giving you a nut." I felt my head jerk back as Tyler pulled me out of the shower by my hair. I felt the glass from the shower going through my thigh. Tyler held on tight to my hair, balled up his fist, and punched me in my face.

"Do you have any idea how much I love you and for you to just throw my love away for some random ass upper-class thug makes me want to kill you, bitch." He punched me three or four more times then let my hair go and started kicking me in my side.

"Tyler, please." He looked down at me, looking like one of those people off the TV show *Fatal Attraction* His ass is a lunatic.

"Tyler please what bitch? You must think it's ok to play with a motherfucka's feelings? This will be the last time you try to fuck over a nigga because this is where your life changes forever."

He punched me in my face again, and my body was burning from being drug through glass. I got the chance to look down at myself and pieces of glass was stuck all over my body. It seemed like I was bleeding from every part of my body.

I could barely move, and my body was hurting so bad. My eyes had started to close from the being punched in the face repeatedly. The nigga standing in front of me was not the Tyler I knew. If I had known he was this crazy, I would have left his ass at hello.

"I bet you'll stay away from that bougie ass nigga now. You're mine bitch, and that will never change."

Tyler continued to beat my ass as I faded in and out. He finally decided to leave after what felt like hours of him beating my ass. My vision was blurred, but I was able to get to my phone, I unlocked the phone with my thumb and hit for Siri.

"Call Bailey."

"Hello," Bailey answered, but I couldn't respond right then. Bailey hung up the phone. I cried then repeated to Siri.

"Call Bailey." The phone rang three times then she picked up.

"Hello!" she said, this time with an attitude.

"Help!"

"What?" I faintly heard Bailey reply before I blacked out.

Sometime later, I felt someone pick me up, and I think I heard Bailey screaming.

❧ 19 ❧

BAILEY

Marcell and I were having a Netflix no chill night. The chill part of it was just getting started when my phone started ringing. It was after three in the morning, and I knew it had to important. No one would call this late unless it was time to dig a hole for a dead body or someone was dying. I stared at the screen seeing it was Khiya and knew it was a problem. I answered the phone.

"Who ass do we have to beat?" She didn't say anything.

"Hello! Hello!" I repeated with an attitude.

She didn't say anything, and that pissed me off because I was in the middle ending my night on a high note. My phone rang again a Marcell was passing me the blunt he had just lit, looking at me like he had an attitude.

"Damn Khiya, I'm trying to suck some dick what bitch." I held the phone to my ear because I heard her breathing hard.

"Bitch, I don't have time to listen while you get your rocks off, especially when I'm trying to get mine off too." Marcell and I laughed until I heard my friend faintly talking.

"Help!" Takhiya whispered through the phone.

I looked at Marcell as I started running to the closet getting my gun. I hadn't said shit to him he just started grabbing his guns and phone. I slipped on my gym shoes, grabbed my car keys, and ran out the door with him on my heels. He pulled out his phone talking to someone as I ran every red light I came upon. I kept calling Takhiya's phone for it to keep going to the voicemail.

"God please let her be ok." I was talking aloud hoping for the best, but I knew in my heart shit was bad. She sounded so helpless on the phone. Whatever happened I know Quan's no good ass had something to with, and I promise I'm shooting him in his dirty ass dick and putting a bullet between his eyes. I kept hitting the phone button on my steering wheel calling Takhiya until was a block away from her house.

I jumped the curve pulling my car up to her front door that was left wide open. Her house was fucked up. Couches were flipped, glass tables were broken, and trash was thrown from the front door to the back.

"You smell gas?" I asked Marcell and went to walk in the kitchen, and Marcell stopped me.

"Go see if Takhiya's upstairs and be careful." I ran up the stairs with my gun in hand and the safety off.

"MARCELL!!!" I screamed at the top of my lungs once I saw my friend on the floor in a pool of blood. I ran over to her, her face was swollen, and she had pieces of glass all over her, with a bigger piece in going through her thigh.

"Khiya, get up baby!" I said, getting on my knees on the side of her.

I laid my head on her chest. Her heart was still beating, but it wasn't strong.

Marcell came in the room

"Damn!" He walked over to her scooping her up in his arms.

"Come on, baby." I took off behind him. He put Takhiya on the back seat of the car. I slid in the back seat and grabbed my phone putting Cook County Hospital in the GPS for him.

"Follow the GPS it's going to take you to her job."

Marcell reversed onto the street and started speeding. He got back on his phone and told whoever to meet us there. I sat in the back seat with tears in my eyes praying for Takhiya. We pulled up to the hospital, and Bryce was standing at the door waiting for us with a worried look on his face. He ran up to the car, picking Takhiya up running in the hospital with her. They grabbed a gurney, and Bryce laid her on it. Nurses and doctors started checking her pulse, sticking shit on her.

"Code blue in the emergency entrance." People started running over to Takhiya.

"Clear!" I started losing my mind. I ran and jumped on top of her.

"Nooo! Khiya, don't do this to me." I felt someone lift me up off her almost immediately.

"Let me go!" I started kicking and screaming. I felt someone wrap their arms around me.

"Calm down Bailey; let them help her." Marcell was softly telling me turning me around to him hugging me. I cried into his chest still hearing them shock Takhiya. I turned to them, and someone was on top of Takhiya giving her CPR as they ran down the hall with her.

"What am I going to do with her? She's my best friend," I cried, standing in the middle of the hallway.

"Don't think like that. She's going to make it out alright." Bryce told me as Marcell hugged me again.

One of the nurses walked up to me handing me a hospital gown.

"Ma'am, do you mind putting this on and taking your weapon to your car." I looked at her like she was crazy.

"Why the fuck do I need to put that on and what gun?" Bryce looked at me with a smirk on his face.

"Bailey, all you have on is your panties and a sports bra, and I hope you have the safety on your gun because your finger has been on the trigger the entire time."

I looked down at myself, and he was right. I ran out the house in nothing but my boy cut short panties and sports bra. I looked down at my hand and put the safety on my gun. I grabbed the hospital gown from the nurse putting it on. When I looked around everyone in the emergency room entrance was looking at me. The men's mouths were hanging open, and one guy was drooling. Marcell wrapped his arm around me and pushed me towards the door. Bryce walked out with us and went to his car. He came over to my car with a t-shirt and jogging pants.

"Where did you get my clothes from?"

"Marcell called me when you walked out the door half naked and asked me to go to your house and get you something to put on." I laughed a little because I walked out my house like this. Then the reason I was outside naked in the first place came to my mind, and I started crying again.

"Marcell pulled a blunt out, lit it, and then handed it to me. Smoke this you need to calm down, Bailey."

I put the blunt to my lips, inhaled the smoke holding it for a minute, then exhaling. I hit it two more times and passed it back to Marcell. I started to calm down and welcome the high. I slipped the pants on that Bryce had gotten me, took off the gown, and put on the t-shirt. Marcell stood there looking at me like I was crazy.

"What nigga?" He pointed to Bryce.

"Your brother has seen my ass as well as seen me act an ass, so why the hell am I covering up now?" He turned to Bryce.

"Turn your head, nigga." I laughed at him.

"Hehehe what the hell are you laughing at? You almost got at least all of them niggas in that hospital shot." He was serious as hell.

I pulled my t-shirt down and walked away from his crazy ass.

We sat in the hospital for eight hours waiting to hear something. Marcus had come by to bring us something to eat. After I ate, I went to sleep. I woke up to Marcell shaking me.

"Are you Bailey Mills?"

"Yes!" The way he looked at me had me in tears before he even spoke."

"Takhiya has suffered a lot of trauma to the body and face. Her nose and two of her ribs are broken. The glass in her thigh went straight through her bone and had to be surgically removed. She's lost a lot of blood, and it's good that we were able to save her baby. Right now we have her in a medically induced coma to give her and the fetus time to recover." My mouth dropped

"Fetus?"

"Yes, she's almost three months pregnant." Turned and looked at Bryce and watched as his eyes bugged out his head.

"A baby?" Bryce repeated.

"Yes nigga, he said baby and almost three months. You do the math; it sounds like that's all you." I then turned to the doctor.

"You all can go see her for about twenty minutes."

I walked off before even getting the room number, going to the elevators. I walked in the room saw her and had to walk back out to get my mind right. She looked so lifeless with all them tubes and shit in her mouth. Her eyes were swollen shut, and she had gauze and tape everywhere from glass going cutting her everywhere. I walked over to her and grabbed her hand.

"Friend, I'm here with you. Even though shit seems bad right now, we're going to make it through this. All I want you to do is stay strong for your baby. Don't worry about shit; I got you." I kissed her forehead because that was the only spot that wasn't taped or bandaged up and walked out the room. Marcell grabbed my hand.

"You ok, baby?"

"Yeah, I'm good."

When we got to my condo, I walked right into the bathroom turned on the shower and broke down crying. I really couldn't believe someone did this to her. After seeing Takhiya, I knew in my heart that LaQuan didn't have anything to do with this. I mean he ain't shit and doesn't know how to treat her, but he loves her too much to brutally beat her like that. I sat thinking about it, and the only name I could come up with was Patrice's bitch ass. For her sake, I hope it wasn't her.

TWO AND A HALF MONTHS LATER

I walked into Takhiya's and kissed her on her forehead like I've done for the last couple of months. I missed my friend so much. You never know how much of your life that a person consumes until they're not a part of it anymore. Don't get me wrong I have faith she would wake up, that's the reason I held on so tight to her. Plus, she's pregnant. It amazed me every day how much her belly had grown. I rubbed her stomach.

"Hey, nephew, although you haven't heard mommy's voice yet know that she loves you more than you can imagine, and so do I." The baby moved under my hand, and I smiled.

"How do you know it's boy?" Bryce said while standing in the door looking at me.

"I just know." He stared at me.

"Did they do another ultrasound?" He came and sat in the chair next to me.

"Yes, but you know every time they try to see if it's a boy or girl the baby turn its back. It's like he wants to surprise y'all."

"Surprise us?" I looked at him.

"Yeah, surprise you and Khiya. I already know what he is so it won't be a shock to me."

"You think she'll be awake by then?" Bryce asked me seriously.

"Hell yeah! When those labor pains get to kicking her in the ass, she'll wake you screaming for pain medicine," I joked.

Truth is I don't know when she's going to wake up. The doctor took her out of the medically induced coma two weeks after she came out of surgery. She just hadn't woke up, but I know that she would. Takhiya's had made it through so much, and this was just another stage in her life she had to pull through by herself. Bryce moved his chair closer to the bed and started rubbing her stomach. It was like the baby knew who he was because every time I saw him do this, the baby would go crazy moving in Takhiya's stomach.

Bryce started telling the baby about its big sister Justice and how she couldn't wait to meet him. As he rubbed her stomach, he continued to talk. We saw her baby's foot clearly through Takhiya's stomach kicking. I walked over to Takhiya and started rubbing her stomach.

"Calm down baby boy; we got you." He kicked harder, and Takhiya sat straight up in the bed. She started coughing hard and swinging on both Bryce and me. Bryce held her down and tried to smooth her while I ran down the hall screaming like a fucking lunatic.

"Help! She's awake! She woke up. We need some help in room 510!" The nurses and a doctor came running in the room to see Bryce holding Takhiya like his life depended on it.

✿ 20 ✿

BRYCE

I was sitting at beside Takhiya while my baby went nuts in her stomach. I watched as Bailey came to over to calm the baby down when fists started flying left and right. I pushed Bailey out of the way, as Takhiya took full swings at me. She must have thought she was still fighting the motherfucka that did this to her. At least I know my baby tried to protect herself, I grabbed her and held her as tight as I could while Bailey ran out the door screaming like a mental patient.

"Calm down, baby. It's me, Bryce. Do you remember who I am?" Once she relaxed in my arms, she finally looked at my face and smiled a little.

"Bailey went to get some doctors and nurses; they'll she'll be right back in shortly." On cue, Bailey walked into the room with tears in her eyes. The nurses and a doctor came in and checked her out.

"Do you know your name?" the doctor asked Takhiya, and she gave everyone's name in the room. She worked with all of them every day for a couple of years.

"Do you know what day it is?" The doctor asked

"Yes! It's August fifth." We all looked around.

"No Takhiya it's October fifteen. Don't panic it's to be expected. We'll have you together and back at work in no time."

"We appreciate all that doc, but Takhiya will no longer be working here." Takhiya looked at me like I had lost my mind.

"And when did you start speaking for me, Bryce."

"Since I found out you were carrying my seed that's when." Takhiya looked around at everyone then looked at her stomach.

"What the fuck? Please. Tell me y'all playing a sick ass joke on me." I stepped back from her.

"Since you're just waking up I'm going to let that slide." Takhiya started crying.

"It's not you Bryce; it's me. How can I be a good mother to child when I don't even know what being a good mother is? My parents were hell on earth, and anything that you could think of that's wrong to do to a child was done to me. This is something that I know I will fuck up, so I don't want to chance it."

I turned my back to her I tried to understand where she was coming from, but I knew God wouldn't be that cruel to do this to me again. I rubbed my hands down my face and walked out of the room. What the fuck am I going to do? It was so hard on me raising Justice by myself. None of this shit was planned, and it's my fault because I shouldn't have been raw doing a bitch I had just met. I walked to the chapel because I needed to have a long talk with the big homie. I walked in and lit a candle for my mom and papi and talked to them and God like they were sitting in the room with me.

I got up and left the chapel feeling better about the situation. I walked to Takhiya's room and saw someone I hadn't seen since the night I wanted to kill him. I stayed back and watched as Tyler interacted with Takhiya and Bailey. When Bailey jumped up, running over to Takhiya, I walked into the room pushing past Tyler. He started to say something, but I cut him off.

"Get the fuck out, or I'll see if you can grow wings." He looked at me like he wanted to say something.

"While you're trying to burn a hole in the back of my head, you need to be beating your fucking feet." Tyler walked out of the room, and I walked towards Takhiya.

"Bryce, please just step out." I could tell from the look on her face she was scared and embarrassed. I turned towards Bailey.

"Just give us a minute, please." I turned my back to walk out the door, and Takhiya hit the floor.

"Bailey, why can't I walk? What's wrong with me?" Takhiya began to cry and laid flat on the floor. I walked over to her lifting her up off the floor putting her in the bed, but I noticed she and the bed were wet. I looked over at Bailey, and she gave me one of those I'll tell you later look.

"Baby, you remember the conversation we had the night we went out." She didn't respond but nodded her head yes.

"I asked you to be my woman. You never gave me an answer, but when my woman is hurting, I find a way to make it better. I've seen you at your worst, and I'm still here. You being my woman, it is my job is to make sure that when you're at your lowest, I get you back to your highest. Don't worry about shit Takhiya; I got you. I don't care if I have to wash your ass, teach you how to become the mother you want to be or kill the next motherfucka to make you happy. We're going to get through this shit together."

I walked her into the bathroom and sat her in a chair.

"Bailey, call the nurse."

I walked out the room looking for that nigga Tyler. Just from Takhiya's reaction from him, I knew he was responsible for this shit. I've always had my suspensions, but I didn't want to move to quick and fuck up. Bailey told me about some bitch named Patrice that Takhiya's ex-nigga used to fuck around with could've done this too. I had been looking for her and the nigga LaQuan, but it was like they had fallen off the face of the earth. One thing I do know though is anyone that fucks with my seed will die a painful ass death. That nigga Tyler was first on my list. He hadn't been in that room not one time while Takhiya was in a coma, now all of sudden he's concerned about her well-being. She pissed all over herself while he was talking to her. I got on the phone with my brothers because we were handling this shit tonight.

I walked back into the room to check on Takhiya. She was sitting in her bed looking a little better.

"How are you feeling?"

"I'm ok now." I sat on the bed next to her wrapping my arms around her.

"Where's Bailey?" She laid her head on my chest getting comfortable.

"She said she had some business to take care of and she would be back tomorrow."

I lifted her head up to look me in my eyes.

"Takhiya, I know you have been through some shit in your life, but I need you to keep it one hundred. What are you planning to do about this pregnancy? It's too late to get an abortion; I don't believe in them anyway. I just want to know are you going to try to be the mother I know you can be or are you going to walk away from us? There's no half-assing shit with me. You can give me my baby, or we can go through this as a team?" She looked at me like I was crazy.

"Bryce, I've been through a lot, and I fear having to take care of someone that can't defend themselves, but there's no way in hell I'm walking away from a child. I know I just woke up and this shit was shocking as hell, but after feeling him move inside me, I know that I will protect him with my last breath." I was relieved as hell to hear that.

"Is there any way possible that Tyler is the father?" She gave me a look like I was dumb.

"I've never slept with him without a condom; this baby is yours." I knew it already, but I just had to ask anyway.

"One more thing, do you know who did this to you?"

"Yes, it was Tyler." That's all I needed to hear. I sat there with her for a couple more hours until she went back to sleep then left.

⚊⚊

I BENT THE BLOCK TO THE ADDRESS THAT MARCELL HAD GIVEN ME while he sat in the passenger seat taking the safety to our guns off.

"You told Pierre and Marcus what we were doing, and they didn't want to come?"

"No, they had some shit to take care of with Natalie, but this ain't nothing."

I parked the car the block behind the house. We walked over to the back of the house, looking through the bushes, only to see Bailey crouched down peeping through the back window. Marcell stepped through the bushes and snatched Bailey's little ass back. She pulled a knife out of nowhere swinging it at his ass. When she turned around and saw who it was, she stopped with her knife in midair. Marcell snatched the knife from her hand and pointed to the car. Once we got in the car, I couldn't hold my laugh in any longer.

"What the fuck is funny nigga and Bailey what the fuck are you doing here?" She looked at him like he had lost his mind.

"The same shit you're doing here, nigga."

"Hell no! Bailey, take you ass home; I'm not going to argue with you about it either."

"Nigga, we're not married, and your name ain't David Mills so you can't possibly be my daddy. I'm going in this house and take care of this shit. You didn't see how scared Takhiya was when that Tyler came in that room. Her face went pale and as dark as she is, you know that's damn near impossible. She was shaking so hard that she pissed on herself. Bryce may feel some sense of responsibility to her, but she is my fucking responsibility. We have years in this shit. She is the sister I've always wanted and nothing is going to stop me from going in this house handling my business."

Bailey's little ass had so much fire in her and was stubborn as hell; she was all in Marcell's face and wasn't backing down for shit. I knew this would eventually get out of hand because Marcell liked for things to go his way, and he was fighting a losing battle.

"Marcell, wrap your hand up and Bailey you have just as much right to be here, I don't really want you here because shit can get ugly, but I'm not going to fight with you."

Bailey smiled, and Marcell looked down at his hand.

"You cut me," Bailey smirked at him and took her gun out taking the safety off.

"You snuck up on me." She walked off, and we followed behind her. When we got to the back door, Bailey picked the lock like she wasn't new to doing it and we walked in the house. The house was completely dark except for the hall light at the top of the stairs. We peeped in the first door at the top of the stairs but stopped when we heard what sounded like a lion roaring coming from the opposite end of the hall. Bailey's eyes got big.

"I wonder how the hell was Takhiya sleeping with this nigga snoring like this at night?"

"Hell, she's not a quiet sleeper herself." Bailey cut her eyes at me.

"Don't come at my friend like that." I smiled at her.

We walked into the room and saw two figures in the bed. I turned on the lights, and the girl lying next to him sat up quickly, but Tyler's ass was still counting sheep.

"Issa man," Bailey dumb ass said after she saw the girl had a thick ass mustache we all couldn't help but laugh. The girl tried to wake Tyler up, and I shook my head at her. This bitch pushed him anyway.

"What bitch, you know I have to get up," was all he got out of his mouth before Bailey jumped on the bed on top of his ass.

The girl in the bed pulled at Bailey trying to get her off him, and Marcell backhanded her so hard that she was an instant knock out. The girl laid on the floor softly snoring while Bailey was smacking Tyler's ass with the gun. I stood in the door watching Bailey's little ass go in. Marcell stood back and was admiring her work too.

"Marcell, you sure you want to fuck with her?"

"Hell yeah; look at my baby go!"

"Naw, you look at her go. Imagine yourself on the other end of that ass whipping if you funk up." He gave me a knowing look.

Tyler finally got a handle on Bailey and threw her up off of him. She looked like Spider-Man on a web the way she jumped back on top of his ass going at him again. I nodded at Marcell, and he walked over to her cautiously.

"Bailey, we need to wrap this shit up. Get off of him."

"You look like you're scared to grab your woman, man." I laughed.

"I'm not trying to get fucked up nigga. You want to try?"

I walked over to Bailey and pulled her off Tyler. She still trying to swing on him and me.

"Take a good look Bryce; this could be you." I laughed at her, but she was serious as hell.

"Laugh all you want, nigga. I don't give a fuck about a boss or mob if you fuck over my girl."

I put her down on her feet walked over to pull Tyler out the bed. Bailey had turned this nigga's face inside and hadn't even shot him yet. Marcell and I tied him and the girl together, and then Marcell threw a bucket of old water over them.

"What the fuck? Untie me so I can beat that lil' bitch ass!" Tyler yelled.

"You're sure you want us to untie you? You might have better luck with one of us than her." I pointed behind me to Bailey.

The girl next to him started crying.

"Sorry baby; you're just at the wrong place at the wrong time." I bent down to take her out of her misery because her crying was getting on my nerves. Hadn't this bitch ever read urban fiction before? Crying wasn't going to help her the bitch had to go. I put my gun close to her head. *POW POW POW!* I jumped back away from her.

"What the fuck?" I turned to Bailey who had the smoking gun.

"You was taking too long, and I didn't like the way that nigga Tyler was looking at me, but you finish home girl. I have no parts in that. I need to get back and check on Khiya." Bailey turned and walked out the room like she hadn't just almost took my head off. Marcell stood there looking at me goofy with a big ass smile on his face.

"I swear I'm going to marry her."

"Marcell, she's going to kill your dumb ass, and I'm not going to fuck with her on that level, trying to retaliate because if we miss, she's killings everyone except the kids."

We finished up and left.

🎔 21 🎔

PATRICE

"Bitch, I'm tired of arguing with you about the same thing every day. I'm a grown ass man I can do whatever the fuck I want." Quan stepped in my face.

"As long as you're living here, you gone do what the fuck I say, and if you're not going to then you can take your chances with them mob niggas that's trying to get in your ass. What the fuck type of nigga that's supposed to be on and have connections in these streets hides out from the next motherfucka? You ain't shit but a punk that's so in love with a half-dead ass bitch that you can't even get on your grind right. You've been living here for three months without bring in a dime, but want me to suck your dick and fuck you only when you want though. You be so off in a zone damn near every time we fucking and you call me that bitch. I have wanted your ass for so long I let the fact that you were moving in with me cloud my judgment. When I first came home from the hospital, I stayed on my knees sucking your dick so much my shit has permanent dents in them. Now you want to run back to that hoe. I hope she dies."

Quan grabbed me by my neck.

"Don't play with Takhiya or me like that. If you ever open your mouth to say some shit like that again... better yet if the thought crosses your mind, I will fucking end your life. Do you understand me?" He kept applying pressure to my neck that it felt like my head was going to explode. My eyes were bucking, and I was trying to talk, but the nigga had a death grip on my ass.

"I said do you understand me?" He really wanted me to answer, but I could breathe let along talk. He finally realized I couldn't respond and let me go, I dropped to the floor, gasping for air as he stood over me.

"Bitch, I said did I make myself clear?" I just nodded my head and while I coughed and tried to catch my breath.

My mother walked into the kitchen.

'I told you multiple times before that he was a no good ass nigga, but no you just had to have him. You thought the world of him and did anything under the sun to get him. Was it worth? That man's heart belongs to another woman. The same woman that he would cheat on to fuck with you and any other female that would let him screw them. You're doing everything to keep this nigga, and you're losing yourself trying to turn into the woman he wants. Shit doesn't go like that baby, just like you love who you love, he does too.

He resents you because he lost her while fucking with you. I'm know you're no angel, and your pussy has more miles on it than my 1984 Chevy Caprice sitting outside, but you're are so much more than he makes you out to be. I know your daddy, God rest his soul, has stood up in his grave looking at the life you're choosing to lead. Now you know I don't like to get in your business, but I know you can do way better than that."

My mom got up and left the kitchen, LaQuan walked in the kitchen with a fresh outfit on. He looked down at the floor like I wasn't shit.

"You a fucking drama queen laying on the floor like somebody done tried to kill you."

"Where the fuck are you going?"

"To mind my motherfucking business, but since you must know I'm going to the hospital to see Takhiya." I jumped off the floor.

"You fresh as fuck in the shit I bought for you. I'll be damned if you go see that bitch in the fit I got for you." He walked up to me and I stepped back quick as hell.

"It's not impossible for me to make you damned." Quan pushed me into the wall

"Bitch, you think you can have what she had, but that shit isn't possible because you will never be the type of woman she is. You're just an average hoe that does average shit to try to keep a nigga like me, but bitch I'm a boss, and I will always want a boss ass bitch beside me."

Quan walked out the door and I sat at the table crying my heart out. All I've wanted in life was this man. When he was with Takhiya, he gave her ass the world even when she was on drugs. When she got with him he was damn near a made nigga, now he's hit rock bottom and I'm here trying to pick his up. He doesn't appreciate that or me. I wish I could let this nigga go, but I can't. It's like he is embedded in my soul, and I don't want anyone but him.

I know y'all think I'm stupid for it, but like my mom said, you can't help who I love. My heart is with him, and I'm going to play my part until he sees the future I see for us. I can't help that I'm the stand by my man type of bitch, but every relationship has its ups and downs. Mines just has more downs than ups. I'm going to get my shit together so that I can be better than that bitch he's called wifey for so long.

I got myself together before I walked past my mother's room. I had to put my plan into action while he was out the house. This nigga wanted better than Takhiya, and he was going to get it. It was nothing wrong with perfecting yourself so that your nigga could be happy.

22

LAQUAN

I can't believe this bitch is acting like a nigga has to bow down to her just because she's been fronting shit for the last couple of months. All the fuck she does is nag a nigga and talk about how I didn't fuck with her because I wanted to fuck with Takhiya. This bitch just don't understand Takhiya is in a breed of her own, and she doesn't wait for the next motherfucka to do shit for her. She's a woman of a different caliber, but this bitch Patrice doesn't even have a caliber to label her to. Or maybe it's just that she has so many that I don't know what the fuck to classify her as. She should be a hoe, thot, hood rat, ratchet, you know it, and she's with it.

I smoked my blunt and pulled up to the hospital, looking around to make sure I as in the clear. I decided to drive around the block to make sure Bailey's car was nowhere I sight before I went in. I put my blunt out and walked into the hospital.

"Yes, I'm here to see Takhiya." Before I could finish her name, the receptionist pulled out a visitors pass.

"She has a lot of visitors daily." She handed me the pass, and I walked to the elevators.

I slowly pushed the door open peeping inside the room, and

Takhiya was sitting up in the bed. She looked good and healthy. Her skin was glowing and just looking at her my dick stood up.

I walked all the way in, and she noticed me. I smiled at her, but the expression she gave me was unwelcoming.

"What the fuck are you doing here, Quan? You know what it doesn't matter just leave." I turned to walk away then fully walked in the door.

"How can you talk to someone you loved like that?"

"When someone that I love took my kindness for weakness, played me like a goofy, and got caught with another nigga mouth on his dick that's how now get the fuck out." I stared at her.

"I came up here because people were saying that you were on your death bed, and I wanted to come see for myself at least ask for forgiveness for the shit I put you through, but fuck you."

"Fuck me for real LaQuan, that's all you've done to me for the longest of time. You were like my gift and my curse wrapped into one. Instead of looking at the fact that I might have outgrown you, and try to man the fuck up yourself, you played me in every way possible. Then to find you with a man that shit almost killed me. Quan, there was nothing in the world that I loved more than you. After I saw that shit, I wanted to take my own life. I hadn't felt that way since the day you told me you would take care of me. How can you tell me that you love me and wouldn't hurt me, but you did it repeatedly?

Yeah we've had good times hell we've had great times, but nothing can compare to the hurt that I've felt only from loving you. I can't do this with you anymore. My life is going in a different direction now, and I'm sorry, but you are not a part of it. I will always love you and appreciate everything you've done for me."

I stood in the doorway with tears in my eyes, Takhiya was right. I had taken her through too much shit, but I thought she would always be there when I done fucking around. I was hurting bad, but I couldn't let her see a real nigga breaking down. I walked over to her bed to hug her. She opened up her arms for me, and as I held her close, I swear I felt moving in her stomach I pulled back.

"You're pregnant?" She held her stomach protectively.

"Yes."

"How many months are you?" She looked down at her hands.

"Six months." I can't believe this bitch wasn't going to tell me that she was having my baby.

"So you hiding whole kids now? You weren't going to tell me that we were having a baby? Bitch, I thought you were different. You are no different than those other hoes in these streets." Takhiya was shaking her head no to me.

"No what?" I was yelling at her.

"This is not your baby, Quan."

"How it's not? We were still together when you got pregnant. You a dirty motherfucka."

"I got pregnant in Miami, Quan. We hadn't had sex for about a month before I left, but if you weren't fucking everything that moves besides me during that time, you would have noticed that!" she screamed at me.

"You know you bogus as hell for that shit, Khiya. I don't give a fuck what I did and who I was doing. How are you going to give my pussy away? Then you let some random ass nigga going in raw and tried to bring that used ass pussy back to me. You out of order ma and you know it."

She pushed herself up out the bed and stood up holding onto the bed. I stepped back because I know if nothing else Takhiya's ass got hands for days and don't give one fuck about beating my ass in this room

"Nigga, your worldwide dick having ass have a lot of nerve, all the shit that you could've and have brought back to me. Nigga, I have loved you through giving me everything, but herpes and HIV. Hoes claiming they're having your baby, and a bitch bringing a baby to my house and calling me every name under the sun because she swore I was the side chick. Let's not forget you fucking Patrice in my house and me finding your right-hand man sucking your dick in our fucking bedroom, Quan. Every bitch you have cheated on me with you have probably went in blind. I've stuck with you through it all because I thought it was love." She took a step towards me and almost fell to the floor. I ran and caught her.

"Leave me the fuck alone, Quan."

"Let me help you." She pushed my hand back.

"I don't need your fucking help, GET OUT!!"

I helped her up and put her in the bed and walked to the door.

"I'm sorry, ma!" She turned her head to the wall, and I walked out the door.

Damn that shit crushed me, she had cheated on nigga, I wanted to beat her ass, but I couldn't because no matter what Takhiya would always be bae. Regardless of who she was with and what she did, I'ma always look out for her.

"You must be lost."

I was so deep in thought I hadn't noticed Bailey standing at the elevator door when it opened to the lobby. I walked out the elevator as she walked in. I pointed my finger at her like it was a gun and heard a gun cock behind me.

"It's too many witnesses here for me to do your ass, but your time is coming soon because we don't take kindly to threats."

The guy walked past me into the elevator, pulling Bailey close to him while keeping his eyes on me. I stood there for a minute trying to figure out where I knew this nigga from. I got in the car, and it hit me that he was one of the niggas that killed Jason and his crew.

"Fuck!" I hit the steering wheel and pulled off. This shit can't be good.

23

TAKHIYA

I walked around the house that Bryce had rented for us until after the baby was born. I was on strict bed rest, and I couldn't travel until the baby was here. The only thing I was supposed to do was stay in bed unless I was going to the bathroom or showering. I had been out of the hospital for two weeks, and Bryce carried me everywhere I went. This bed rest shit got old quick, and I just needed some air. I was being waited on for everything. I couldn't even open my eyes without someone being there asking me am I ok.

I had to do light therapy for my leg, but if Bryce thought I was doing too much with that, he stopped it. He's put my physical therapist out of the house more times than I count within these two weeks. The reason I was out of the bed now was because he was registering Justice for school and I sent the maid to the store for some chocolate ice cream and salt and vinegar chips. These damn cravings be killing me, and if I can't get what I want, I have an issue with everyone in the house except Justice.

In such a small amount of time, I have fallen in love with her. She's so helpful, smart, and very pretty. Bryce has done a great job in raising her by himself. You would think with him doing what he does for a living that she would be a brat. Being around Justice has me so excited to have my own little one. I rubbed my stomach as I felt my little one moving around, my baby was so active already, and he goes crazy when Bryce is close.

"Mrs. Mariano, what are you doing out of bed?" I could tell Bryce was irritated, but I didn't care. He couldn't keep me locked in our room.

"Bryce, I'm tired of sitting in that room all day. All I can do is lay in the bed, and I'm tired of it. I've laid in a bed for three months prior to this. You have to let me get some air sometimes." He scooped me up in his arms giving me a kiss on the lips.

"Are you trying to kill our baby?"

"Now you know that's the last thing I want to do, I just want out of that room Bryce." He sat me on the bed giving me another kiss.

"Ok babe, we're going to make and agreement. If you promise to stay in the room and get catered to like the queen you are, I will give the D once a week." I thought about it.

"No deal." The doctor said that we could have sex regularly as long as it wasn't rough and I controlled the depth, but Bryce was taking shit to the extreme. He told me if I needed bed rest than he wasn't laying pipe because he didn't want shit to go wrong.

"What do you mean no deal? As hot as your horny ass is that should be enough."

"Bryce, my hormones have been passed out of control, and you've taken and found all of the toys that I begged Bailey to buy me. Now you think dick once a week is supposed to keep me at bay. Hell no! I need it at least five days out of the week to be happy."

"How about twice a week or I fire the maid for leaving you in the house by yourself and lock you in the room when I leave the house." This nigga was driving a hard bargain, and he knew I like Maria, but I had to call his bluff.

"Fuck Maria; she doesn't let me eat pickles anyway. What about sex for three days and the other four you give me some head?" He laughed at me.

"Deal." I was so happy to hear that I hadn't paid attention to him stripping my clothes off until his tongue dove inside my pussy.

"Yes, baby."

Bryce started eating my pussy so good that I knew he missed this just as much as I did. He took his time while he was down there. He moved his tongue to my clit and stuck two fingers inside of me. My body began to react immediately. I was shaking and squirting him his mouth in no time. He didn't stop though he kept sucking and licking and teasing until I was screaming his name. He stripped his clothes off and slowly started giving me the dick inch by inch. He got all the way in then pulled halfway out and rolled his hips a little, making me go crazy. I started rolling my hips and pushing myself down to get more of the dick, but he stopped mid-stroke.

"See that's why I won't let you get on to you have no control, be still and let me do this. You know my dick is far from little, you will get enough." I rolled my eyes at him.

He sank back in my pussy and exhaled loudly. I started working my muscles on him, and he started to lose it. It was like this nigga forgot everything he said about my hot ass, but fuck it; I went along with it and welcomed all that D. I started rolling my hips while working my muscles, and he went in a little too hard. He got over me and slowed down. He slapped me on my hip and gave me the rest of the dick. I was coming back to back.

"Give me what I like seeing baby, you know what I like."

On command, I started squirting all over him.

"Yeah baby, that's it."

The baby started going crazy, I then felt it kick down my pussy, and Bryce was pulling out mad as hell.

"Your baby just kicked my dick." I started laughing because he was seriously mad.

"We have to talk to this baby about respect because it has none." I laughed even harder as he walked to into the bathroom. He came back with a bowl of water and a towel washing me up.

"No sex for you until you teach your child some manners, I pray he's a boy so I can thump his little baby nuts to see if he likes it." I laughed so hard at him.

When Bryce was done washing me up, I laid back and thought back to two weeks ago when he brought me home.

"This is not the way to my house, Bryce."

"*I know ma; I have something for you.*" *We pulled up to a church Justice walked out the door with Marcell and Bailey.*

"*What's going on?*"

"*Look ma; I know shit has been happening fast between us and we haven't had any real time to get to know each other. One thing I do know is that a nigga doesn't want to go another day without tying you to me. From the first day I saw you in that elevator, I knew I had to have you, and I was going to get you. You almost lost me, and I almost lost you and my seed. So from here on out, I want to keep you close.*" *He pulled out a five-carat princess cut diamond ring.*

"*How close do you want to keep me, ma?*"

My eyes started watering, and I couldn't catch my breath. All this time I thought it would be Quan and me doing this, and it's so crazy how another man can see what he wants in a matter of months and come and get it.

"*What's it gone be, ma?*"

"*Yes, baby!*" *He slid the ring on my finger kissing me then got out of the car walking around to get me out. Before he opened the door, he looked at his three brothers and Bailey.*

"*She said yes.*" *Everyone smile and congratulated him, except Pierre.*

"*Good, now we won't have to kill her.*" *Everyone turned to look at him. Bryce picked me up, walking up the stairs. I looked down at him.*

"*What the hell did Pierre mean by that?*" *Bryce kissed my forehead.*

"*Don't worry about him, baby. We weren't going to kill you, but it might have been a shotgun wedding.*" *He laughed, but I didn't see shit funny. What the hell am I getting myself into?*

Bryce carried me to the back to get changed Bailey and Justice followed close behind us. Bryce kissed me one more time and stepped out of the room as Bailey pulled a simple cream Gucci evening gown out. She pulled out a box with some bad ass gold Gucci five inch Stilettos that had a strap around the ankle.

"*Bailey, I can't walk in those.*" *She smiled at me.*

"*Who said you were walking? Just because you can't stand up and flaunt in these bitches doesn't mean that you still can't sport them. Don't worry Khiya, Bryce and I have everything together for you. Just chill and get catered to.*"

About twelve people rushed into the room at one time. In no time Bailey, Justice, and I had people all over us. One person in our head, on our hands, feet, and face all at one time. It felt like hours had passed, and I was getting nervous. Justice patted me on the leg.

"Khiya, are you going to be my new mommy?" Tears came to my eyes. Justice was so young but smart. I looked down into her expectant eyes as she looked back at me waiting for my answer.

"Yes, baby. I'm going to be your new mommy if it's ok with you?"

"Of course it is. I like you." I laughed at her as tears rolled down my face.

"You're messing up your makeup Khiya, and the last thing you want is to walking down to your future husband looking like a raccoon." I laughed at her.

"I'm ok."

I wiped my eyes, and the makeup artist reapplied some of my makeup. Once everything was done, I looked into the mirror and smiled. I know Bryce paid a lot of money for these people to come out because when I first got here, I looked tore up but these people have a bitch looking like a billion bucks, fuck a million. My glam squad cleared out, and I looked at all of us. Bailey had on a gold dress similar to the one I had on without the train and cream Gucci stilettos, but the heel of her shoes was gold. Justice looked beautiful in her gold and cream little puffy dress with her little train on the back. Her hair hung down her back in huge spiral curls. She had on cream tights with little cream socks with the gold ruffle trim, and her little gold Gucci shoes finished off her dress.

There was a knock on the door. Marcell and Pierre walked in looking handsome in their cream Gucci suits and gold cuff links.

"You ladies ready?" Marcell asked us while picking Justice kissing her on the cheek.

"Hey, Uncle Marcell and Pierre you look pretty."

"No baby, I'm handsome your Uncle Marcell and Marcus are pretty." She raised her eyebrow at him.

"Men are handsome baby and pretty is used for girls," Marcell corrected her.

"Let's get this disaster waiting to happen on the road." We all stopped looking at Pierre.

"Why are you always so negative?" Bailey asked. Pierre just looked at her.

"Wait, I'm missing my something borrowed." Marcell put Justice down.

"Baby, go wait at the doors for us." Justice grabbed her flower basket and ran out the room. Marcell reached under his jacket and handed me a big ass gun.

"Here, I know it's not traditional, but nothing about this wedding is right know. You can't walk down the aisle, so Pierre is going to carry you. If that nigga act like he's going to drop you, shoot his ass."

I happily grabbed the gun, and when Pierre picked me up, I put it in my lap.

I watched as Marcell and Bailey walked down the aisle to "Halo" by Beyoncé when they got to the altar, and Justice stepped out to drop the petals to the lilies the music changed to "If This World Was Mine" by Luther Vandross.

When Justice got to the middle of the aisle before Pierre stepped out, he looked at me.

"Takhiya, if you hurt my brother the way the last bitch did, I swear on my parents you will die a slow and painful death." He started to walk out.

"Hold on. First, off nigga, I'm not the next bitch, and before you began to judge me on some shit your heartless ass will never understand, get all the facts. I'm not here to hurt anyone including your evil ass but never underestimate the underdog nigga. Now take me to my husband."

Pierre started walking down the aisle, and I could tell by the looks on Marcell and Bailey's faces that they knew something went down. I looked past them to my future husband and everything I had been through faded away.

I know that we hadn't known each other that long, but all this just felt so right. Bryce was so happy, and the smile on his face made me smile just as hard. As we got closer to him, my heart rate picked up, and I knew right then that whatever it took to be the wife of a mob boss I was willing to do. This was the beginning of my new life with my new family, and I knew that I would go to war for them and kill a motherfucka if I had to. I knew this right here was the love that I've always wanted. Everything was falling into place for me. I was having a baby, a beautiful five-year-old, and my husband that I would give my life for. We made it to the front, and I was in front of Bryce. He couldn't wait for the ceremony to start before he kissed me.

"I know y'all don't think I'm holding her fat ass through the whole thing, I just carried her big ass down the aisle."

"Knock his ass out with that gun, Khiya." Bailey grabbed the chair from behind her, placing it in front of Bryce.

"I can stand on my own two feet," I told all them.

"Then you should've walked down the fucking aisle then," Pierre said I rolled my eyes at him, and the priest cleared his throat.

"We are still in the house of God."

Pierre sat me in the chair, and I kept the gun in my lap. The priest looked down at me.

"Do you really need that here? We are all safe in the house of the Lord."

"Sorry it's my something borrowed; we had to improvise." Marcell started

laughing, and to make the man of God feel safe, I handed the gun to Bailey with my bouquet.

"Dearly beloved we are gathered here today to join Bryce and Takhiya in holy matrimony. Is there anyone here that objects to this union?" I reached my hand back up to Bailey to give me the gun back while looking at Pierre. Everyone started laughing, but I was dead ass. Once no one objected, the priest continued with the service.

"I now pronounce you Mr. and Mrs. Mariano; you may kiss the bride." I kissed Bryce with everything in me. I know this mob shit won't be easy, but I was willing to put my best foot forward.

24

BRYCE

I sat in my office listening to everything Pierre was telling me about the shipment that my people got jacked for. I wasn't happy about losing five million dollars, and someone was going to pay for this shit. I can't believe motherfuckas could be so incompetent and take food out of their own families mouths.

"Bryce, we need to handle this. I understand you have to look out for your wife and Justice, but they will be safe here. We could have Marcus stay here and watch after them while you, me, and Marcell go take care of everything." I looked at all my brothers as they stared back at me.

"Marcus are you cool with Pierre's plan?"

"Do I have a choice in this matter?"

"Yes, every one of us has choices in this, but I would prefer if one of us stayed here. It can't be Pierre or me, so you and Marcell can flip or coin or play rock, paper, scissors. I don't care how y'all handle it, but someone needs to keep an eye on my wife and Justice," I replied to Marcus.

"What about Bailey? Marcell, how are things going with that LaQuan shit?" Marcell wiped his hands down his face.

"We already know Bailey can take care of herself, but everything has been quiet with LaQuan since that day at the hospital."

"I'll just stay. Justice likes me better than Pierre and Marcell anyway. Marcell if y'all are going to be gone for a while maybe you should have Bailey stay here with us." Marcus smirked at Marcell.

"Man bruhs don't be trying to push up on my woman while I'm gone. You had your chance and blew it. Don't make me fuck you up, bro." Marcus laughed.

"You're scared of a little competition?" Marcell stood up.

"You're my brother, and I love you, but I'm not above shooting your ass in the foot. Any of these other hoes I wouldn't give a fuck about, but Bailey is wifey and don't forget that shit." Marcell sat down after proving his point.

"It's settled then; we leave tonight."

I walked in the room that Takhiya had been living in for the last couple of weeks.

"Tee, where you at?" I walked further into the room.

"The only place you allow me to go by myself. I busted in the bathroom and regretted it as soon as the smell hit my nose.

"And I would like to have some peace while I'm in here."

"Damn girl, what the hell you been eating? You should be ashamed of yourself."

"You can leave out of here anytime you're ready, and I didn't smell like this until you hired a fucking maid that couldn't cook." Here we go with this shit again.

"You're just mad you let your mouth overload your ass and really didn't think I would fire Maria. If you would have stayed in bed when you sent her to the store, she would still be here. Maria losing her job is on you, not me."

I sprayed some air freshener and closed the bathroom door fast as hell. I sprayed the room after that. When I get back home, the first thing I will do is hire another maid. Takhiya smelled so bad that if I had lit a match, the entire house would have gone up. Takhiya wobbled out of the bathroom, looking at me, and I could tell she was in rare form. Her pregnancy was taking me through it. Sometime she would be nice and mellow, while other times she was as mean as a junkyard dog. I really had to step lightly around her. She walked over to the bed and sat down. I rubbed her belly and kissed her.

"Tee, I have to go out of town for a couple of days." She looked at me.

"Why? What about Justice and me?"

"Tee, I really have been taking shit light with you, fucking with comes at a cost. Me leaving for a couple of days is nothing compared to the shit that could be happening. I have uprooted my life to be here with you until my baby is born. I have to go to Miami, but I'm leaving Marcus here with you and Justice. Don't give him a hard time and don't do anything that can fuck you or the baby up." She smacked her lips and rolled her eyes at me.

I got up and started packing , and she watched me as I moved around the room and huffed every now and then.

"If you promise me you'll be good, I'll call Maria and tell her to be here by the time you wake up." She sat back and pulled the covers over her legs before I walked out I handed her the credit card I had ordered for her.

"Here Tee, order whatever you want you want for you and the kids. I'll be back as soon as I can." Her eyes beamed at the credit card, and I knew she was going to put a dent in my account before I was out of the house good. I gave her kiss and walked out the door.

MIAMI

We got off our private jet and walked right to the limo. Instead of going to the house, I told the driver to take us to Mariano's. I hadn't been home in over three months, so I had to check on our baby. The club was one of several business ventures that we have, but I put a lot of work into this one.

We walked in the door of the club and Jasmine was standing there with a huge smile on her face.

"Hey fellas." She gave all of us a hug but held on to me a little longer.

"Hey." We all replied to her, and I stepped away from her.

"If I would have known you were coming home we could have celebrated the right way."

As soon as my brothers turned their backs, she grabbed a hand full of my dick. I stepped back as my dick began to get hard. I know I'm married, but hell, I'm a man before anything. Marcell and Pierre walked into the crowd, and I went up to my office with Jasmine in tow. I walked right to my desk.

"How's everything been going here?" She started stripping out of her clothes.

"Wait, Jasmine. Before this gets any further, I'm a married man now, and it's a lot of shit I may do in this world, but cheating on my wife isn't one of them. Put your clothes back on because the only thing we can discuss or handle with each other is business. If you decide that we can't work together any longer, I can understand that. If you decide to stay then no that yo will respect everything concerning my marriage." Jasmine pulled her shirt back on, and Olivia busted in my office.

"How the fuck did you know I was back?"

"I didn't know you had left until I came to the house with my father so that he could see Justice. Where the fuck is my child, Bryce?" I laughed so hard at her tears came to my eye.

"What child? Do I have a child with you?"

"Stop fucking playing me. Bryce, you know damn well that Justice is mine."

"I know that you gave birth to a beautiful little girl and bailed on her before she had a name. Now, what do you and your father want with my child?"

"You know he's in his last days, and he wants to spend some time with her before he dies."

"He should have thought about that before the both of you decided to disown her. We've been having this conversation for five years now, and personally, I'm tired of it. I don't think it's fair to Justice for her grandfather to get to know her just to die on her weeks later. Who's going to console her after that? Have either of you thought about that? You and your father are selfish for this. I'm not going to send my child through this and with him being a father himself I know he will understand."

"You selfish son of a..."

"Call my mother a bitch if you want to and you will be picking your teeth off the floor. The only reason I haven't tried to put your ass in the grave is because I thought one day my daughter may want to meet the woman that has never had time for her. Since my wife has shown her more affection in a matter of months than you have in her entire life, and one of them she was in the fucking hospital, I feel like she really doesn't need you anymore. But since the only love you feel is for your father I think I'ma have fun watching you suffer." Olivia stomped her foot then picked up a chair, throwing it at me.

"You have a fucking wife? You dirty bastard. You said you would love me forever. Not only that, but you have some bitch around my child."

"Olivia give up, all of it. We are not together; forever ended five years ago, and you knew damn well I wasn't going to take you back." Olivia walked over to Jasmine, who I had forgotten was in the office while Olivia and I were arguing. Olivia charged at Jasmine.

"I wanted to beat your ass some months ago, but I guess since you have taken my life from me, I have more of a motive now." Jasmine turned sideways and kicked Olivia hard in her stomach.

"Not today bitch, and by the way, I'm not his wife." Olivia was flat on her back with her arms holding her stomach. Jasmine looked down at her one more time and walked out the office door.

I didn't come to Miami for this shit. Olivia has always been a pain in my ass. I walked over to her bending do to help her up. I didn't say a word to her; I just open the door. She walked to the other side of the door.

"Bryce, I swear on my mother's grave."

I slammed the door in her face. I didn't have time for any of this shit. I went back and sat at my desk. My phone rang letting me know it was time to take care of business. Everything was in good time so that I could get this over with and get back to my girls.

I let my brothers know it was time to go.

WE PULLED UP TO ONE OF MY WORKER'S HOUSES, NOT REALLY knowing what to expect.

"This nigga is living good, I know we pay everybody well, but damn. Carlos is living better than us."

I looked at the huge mansion that he had bought a couple of days ago off my dime, I and instantly became pissed. We all pulled out our guns, and Pierre kicked the door in, I saw someone try to run up the stairs and fired hitting them in the leg.

"Damn, don't do me like this. I have my wife and kids in the house."

"Who knew we would luck up and find this nigga as soon as we got in here." I looked over at Marcell as he spoke and then down at Carlos as he cried and begged us not to kill his family.

"I just moved here. I think you have the wrong person. Don't kill me, man."

I moved into the light so he could see who he was talking to right before I hit his ass in the head with my gun, knocking him out. I heard footsteps and looked at the top of the stairs to see a woman coming down I pointed my gun at her.

"Make one more move, and I swear I will make your kids orphans."

"What are you doing to my husband?" Marcell pointed his gun at her.

"Look lady; we are trying to let you live, but you're making this shit real hard for a nigga. Your husband has touched some shit that didn't belong to him, so now he has to pay the price for this shit. You keep this shit up, and you and your kids will pay for his transgressions too. Go back to your room and go the fuck to sleep. If you decide to call the police, I will come back here and dismember your fucking kids in front of you. Think about that shit while you're dreaming about planning Carlos funeral."

Pierre and Marcell picked Carlos up and put him in the trunk of the car. Carlos would be nothing but a memory in a little while, but I had to see who helped him steal our product and money. I know his dumb ass didn't do this alone, he was just the stupid motherfucka that got caught first.

"Don't think we're going to be doing all the fucking heavy lifting, nigga. I understand you're over the family and shit, but you are going to get your hands dirty too." Marcell ass always had to be the one to all the most shit.

"I'm older than you, so I say you carry him." I pulled the same shit he used to pull with Marcus all the time.

"I'm older than both of y'all so I'm not doing shit but supervising carry that nigga into the building."

We had pulled up to our warehouse, and I was glad because Carlos was in the trunk acting a fool. We got out the car, and as soon as Pierre popped the trunk, Marcell hit Carlos with the gun knocking him back out. Marcell and I carried Carlos in the building and tied him to the chair. Pierre smacked Carlos so hard he woke up.

"What in the hell?"

"Hell is right, you are in hell, and while you're here, you will suffer until I get the information I need from you. Why did you steal our money and who helped you."

"Man Bryce, I will never do that to y'all man. Y'all have always looked out for your workers I wouldn't do y'all like that man." Carlos' eyes were pleading with me, but I can't believe this nigga would lie to me with a straight face. I nodded towards Pierre, and he pulled his gun out and shot Carlos in his other leg.

"Feel like talking now?"

"I swear on my kids man."

I nodded at Pierre again, and he walked behind him and shot through his hands. Afterwards, he took some bleach and poured it on his hands. Carlos screamed at the top of his lungs. Pierre smiled being satisfied with his work.

"Carlos, you have a lot of body parts, and I'm sure Pierre can think of more fucked up ways to make you scream enough, but I don't have all day to play with." I pulled out my gun and shot him in his dick then put my gun to his head. I smelled his flesh burn from the hot metal touching his skin.

"Marcell?" When I called his name, he turned on a blow torch.

"It was David. Please let me go I won't say anything to anyone." I put a bullet in his head and called the cleanup crew. I walked out mad as hell. David was my best friend and right-hand man. He took care of everything when we couldn't. I made sure he was very well paid because he had a lot on his plate.

"I told you we should have gotten rid of his ass when we took care of his cousin for fucking up the product with those Chicago niggas. I knew it was going to be some shit Bryce, and I told you to let me do them both. I know y'all have been what ma called birth buddies, but fuck that. It's like a nigga that I work for killing one of y'all and he thinks I'm not coming after him. You should have known he was going to find out it was us."

Pierre was right I should've known better. I thought I had put together the perfect plan when we killed John in the drive-by in Englewood. They do that shit on a regular, so I wasn't worried about the backlash from David. I guess I was wrong though.

"That's your friend, so that's your problem," Marcell finally spoke.

We walked to the car knowing it was going to be a long night. We pulled up to David's house, and I used my key to go in. I maneuvered through the dark remembering the entire layout of the house. I twisted my silencer on the gun and walked into the room that David shared with his wife. They both slept peacefully not knowing that tomorrow they would be waking up next God.

"What took you so long, bro?"

"No, why would you do this to me? We have been through everything together for you to fuck me over."

"Family is everything, and you know that? You killed my cousin. We grew up like brothers. We may have grown apart as we got older, but he was still my blood. My auntie has been blaming me for this shit since you killed him. This shit was eating me alive, and I knew the only way to get to you is to fuck with your money. I don't give a fuck if I live or die my wife and kids are good for life."

"Wrong again nigga; your kids are good for life."

David tried to jump up, but I put a bullet through his head faster than he could move. I turned to Deanna and put a bullet through her head too. Deanna ain't the kind of bitch you let live. She's a real ride or die chick that would kill everyone except Justice, then turn around and raise my daughter like she was her own. I felt bad because my godkids will need me soon, and I'll have to caress their feelings knowing I'm the one that caused them pain. I turned to walk out the door, and my brothers were at the door waiting for me.

"Come on. Let's go, man."

Although I lost my best friend tonight, I knew that my brothers would be here with me forever.

❧ 25 ❧

BAILEY

Marcell hadn't even been gone twenty-four hours, and I missed him already. Since the brothers decided to stay in Chicago for a while, Marcell and I have gotten close. He has practically been living with me. There was only one night that he didn't come in, but he has been here every night since.

The night of Bryce's and Takhiya's wedding, Marcell and I decided to get a room at the Hilton downtown. When we checked in the front desk clerk was flirting her ass off with Marcell like I wasn't standing next to him.

"Instead of flirting with my man, you need to be getting our room key."

This white hoe gave me one of those privileged ass laughs like find your place you little whore. She rolled her eyes and kept talking like I was a figment of her imagination. She stood there and quoted her number to Marcell. As we were walking off, I turned around to go snatch her ass up and imagine my surprise when she steps from behind the desk and is thick fuck. This bitch was a brick house shit, and I personally wanted to fuck her ass, and I don't even do women. Marcell turned around to get me and stopped in his tracks looking at her.

I turned around to him.

"Close your mouth nigga, let's go." Long story short we stay the night at the hotel, but the next day Marcell phone is going off like crazy.

"Who is that blowing you up like that?"

"I don't know the number, so I haven't been answering it." I looked down at his phone, and it was that bitch.

"Hey love you must want to fuck my boyfriend and me because that's the only way you're getting a piece of that dick. Understand baby if he fucks I fuck. Now lose his number before I call your job and let them know you're going through customers information. Bye bitch."

I hung up the phone just for her to start calling again. I went to the bathroom to shower. When I got out, I noticed the phone hadn't rung at all. Around seven-thirty that evening Marcell got up to leave. Now I'm far from insecure, but I knew some shit was off. I tried to shake it off, but I couldn't woman's intuition is a motherfucka. I got up to put on my clothes and picked my gun up. Most people would think I'm stupid for this, but I'm not. I have to prove a point to Marcell and this bitch.

First one is being disrespectful can get you killed and the second one is for Marcell's ass. If you with me I'm the only bitch you're fucking. I got in my car, tracked his iPhone, and took off. This bitch thought she was slick; she had booked the same room we had the previous night. I was heated. I clipped the janitor's key card as I walked past him. I opened the door. Marcell was sitting on the bed, and this bitch was on her knees about to put his dick in her mouth.

"Marcell!" He jumped off the bed knocking homegirl on the floor. I pulled my gun up and she bout like fainted.

"I knew she was one of those street people." This bitch had the audacity to say. I pointed my nine with the silencer on it at her and grazed her foot.

"Bitch, next time I will aim a little higher and stop all that crying and screaming and shit before I put one between your eyes. As for you Marcell, did I or did I not tell you don't make me fall in love and try to cross me?"

Even being in my mid-twenties, I had never fallen in love until I started fucking with Marcell. I had told him before we had gotten this serious that I had never been in love so if I was hurt, I didn't know what lines I would cross. Hint: I'm in the fucking Hilton in downtown Chicago shooting at this nigga and crying ass bitch.

I shot at Marcell missing each time I wasn't trying to hit him. I just wanted his ass to get the memo. After I shot at him the third time, he walked over to me snatching my gun away from me.

"That's enough with your crazy ass, Bailey damn. I got your point you're in love with me, and if I leave you or hurt you, you will kill me."

"No nigga I will shoot you not kill you, but if you try to cheat on me again, I'm going to Lorena Bobbit your ass. You got it?" Marcell grabbed his dick flinching then kissed me.

"You're just going to leave me like this?"

"Bitch, it's either leave you like this or leave you in the morgue, which one would you like?" I replied quickly turning to point my gun at her.

"That's what I thought," I said as she sat there silent, I threw the keycard on the floor and walked out with Marcell in front of me.

Damn, I missed the shit out of him. I laid on the bed playing with my pussy and sending Marcell pictures of it.

Bailey: You like that, daddy?

Marcell: Yes. I see you wet for daddy. Stick another finger all the way in.

I got tired of going back and forth with his ass and getting pussy juices all over my phone. I sat my phone on the dresser grabbed my bullet and Face Timed him. He picked up on the first ring, and I was ready to bust my first nut.

"I'm coming, daddy."

"Yes, baby come let that pussy talk to me.

I started playing with my pussy more so that he could hear her talking back to him. This shit was feeling so good to me.

"Baby, she's about to come for you again." I felt it. I was coming hard two seconds later I was squirting across the room.

"There it goes ma, exactly the way I like her." I looked at the phone and Marcell was licking his sexy ass lips like he was ready to catch all of me. I laid there playing with my pussy some more and kept squirting.

"Damn ma you in rare form tonight, but daddy will be home sooner than you think."

"Babe, look behind you." Marcell was so into the show I was putting on for him that he didn't feel Pierre's nosy ass standing behind him.

"Nigga, are you looking at my woman?" Marcell had turned the phone upside down, and all could do was listen to him curse Pierre out.

POW! BOOM!

"What was that, Bailey?"

I jumped my naked ass out of bed picking up my phone and grabbing my gun running to the door. I opened the door to see LaQuan cutting ass to get to the stairs. Marcus came from the opposite side of me falling in my arms.

"NOOOO!!!" I screamed at the top of lungs looking down at Marcus, and my heart was breaking by the second. He had a big ass hole in his chest going through to his back.

"What the fuck is going on, Bailey? Talk to me?" I heard Marcell yelling through the phone that had fallen to the floor.

"Marcus, hold on for me baby." His eyes were still open I picked the phone up.

"Babe, LaQuan shot Marcus. I'm going to call you back." I hung and called the police while holding him in my arms.

"I got you, baby, just stay with me." Marcus looked up at me.

"Damn Bai, you bad as hell." Those were the last words he said to me before he took his last breath.

I grabbed my phone as the paramedics ran to us and did CPR on Marcus getting him back and rushing him out the building. I got up throwing on anything I could find and got in my car. I call Takhiya to meet me at the hospital.

I ran into the hospital, and Takhiya was already there crying her eyes out holding on to Justice as she cried into her chest. I walked over to them.

"Have you called the brothers?" Takhiya shook her head no.

The last thing I wanted to do was make this phone call, but Takhiya was taking care of Justice and drowning in her own sorrow right now. I got myself together pulled out my phone and made the call I was dreading to make.

"Yeah babe, are you sitting down?"

❧ 26 ❧

MARCELL

I jumped up running to the living room.

"Come we have to go, Marcus has been shot."

Bryce and Pierre jumped up. I grabbed the car keys and sped to the airport. It took twenty minutes to get there, and it felt like hours. We all ran to the jet. My phone started ringing, and I knew this shit was all bad. I felt the disconnection from Marcus on the drive to the jet. I just didn't want to believe that my brother was gone. We were damn near twins exactly nine months to the day apart. I answered the phone.

"He's gone."

"Yes, babe!" I was really asking her because I knew it already, but hearing her confirm what I already knew fucked me up. This pain was worse than my parents leaving. My twin was gone, and all I could do was drop to my knees.

"He didn't make it," was all I could say before I broke down in the worst way.

I couldn't help my brothers in what they were feeling; I couldn't do shit because the pain I felt had paralyzed me. I felt my brothers helping me up into the chair for takeoff, but I was out of it. It felt like I lost my other half. It was more than a piece of me missing. I was in a daze the entire ride to Chicago. When I walked into the hospital I had tunnel vision, Bailey was talking to me, but it sounded like the boy on the show *Charlie Brown* talking.

We all walked to the morgue, and when I saw Marcus on the screen, I lost my fucking my mind. I thought about Bryce telling me that it was LaQuan that killed him, I grabbed Bailey by her neck and slammed her against the wall hard.

"It's your fucking fault bitch; my brother is gone because he came to check on you. All he was doing was what I asked him to do. Why did he have to like this, over some pussy? He's gone, and bitch you're going to leave with him."

I applied more pressure to her neck, and tears rolled down her face as she tried to swing on me. Takhiya and Justice were screaming, and my brothers were trying to pry my hands off of her. Bailey's lips started to turn blue when everything just faded.

I woke up in one of the hospital beds with a banging ass headache. Everyone was in the room with me, including Bailey. I looked at her, and she held her head down. When she looked back up at me, I saw the handprints around her neck. I felt bad for doing that to her, I love the shit out of this woman, but I was lashing out and found one the only person in the room that I could hurt. The pain was unbearable after losing my brother, but hurting my girl made me feel even worst.

"I need you Bailey, please don't leave me. You're the only one that can help me through this. I'm sorry!" I know it's not good for a real nigga to go soft like that, but no one is in here but my family.

"Please say something, Bai." I watched the tears roll down her face as she put her hand on her neck and kind of flinched.

"Ok!" It came out of her mouth so softly. I had choked my baby so bad that she could barely speak, but she found it in her heart to forgive me.

"I wouldn't be so content with her saying ok. She may still beat the shit out of you and put you back in here for this stunt you pulled," Bryce said, and we all laughed a little, but when I looked around the room not seeing Marcus fucked me up again. I might have gone off on their ass again, but my head was hurting so bad.

"What happened to me? Why is my head hurting so bad?"

"Your head is hurting because my wife hit you in the back of your head with my gun." I turned to Takhiya that sat there with a careless expression on her face.

"You were hurting my friend don't expect a sorry from me, deal with it." Takhiya got up and waddled to the bathroom.

I looked around the room at who I had left. Every person in here had a place in my heart I wasn't letting anyone else be taking from me again. I'm going to protect them until I take my last breath. The first thing I'm going to when all this shit is over is take care of LaQuan and anyone that gets in my way.

27

BRYCE

The days have gone by in a blur. I can't believe my baby brother is gone. I sat on the couch thinking about all the shit my brothers, and I had gone through. I couldn't describe the emotions that I was feeling because we have had good times and bad. All of us were going through a thing because while we were killing someone else's brother, ours was being taken away from us. I felt so bad for Marcell and Bailey because they were taking it harder than all of all us. I went to check them yesterday, and I could feel the distance between them. Bailey said she just keeps dreaming of him falling in arms taking his last breath and Marcell is taking it harder than all of us because he and Marcus had this weird ass connection. I can tell that he has a void spot in him.

Marcell has a problem with lashing out, and I feel like he's going to take it out on the wrong person again. I held my own personal resentment against my wife, but I had to watch my encounters with her. I just lost my brother, and I don't know what I would do if my actions towards her caused her to lose my baby. I tried to stay away from her as much as possible, but all I keep thinking is if we never stayed in Chicago, Marcus would be alive and dying to smash the next bad bitch he seen.

Takhiya was taking Marcus death kind of hard and all she wanted to do was be there for me. Like I said though, I feel like my actions concerning her is what has us morning my brother now. My poor baby Justice didn't know what to do, Marcus was her favorite uncle. Every night Takhiya and I had to sit in her room and practically rock my baby to sleep. She would just break down and cry if she saw a pair of his shoes in the house. With Marcus being the baby boy and us relocating to Chicago short term, Marcus would just stay between the three of our houses. He was at my house more than any of the other brothers because I had the most room, and he loved being around Justice.

Justice ran into the room sitting on my lap.

"Daddy, after today I won't get a chance to see Uncle Marcus anymore?"

"No baby! Uncle Marcus is going to be with your nana and nonno."

"How am I supposed to remember him?" I was on the brink of tears, but there was no way I could let my baby girl see me break down.

"We have tons of pictures and videos that we have of him, baby."

I pulled out my phone and found the video of Justice's birthday from earlier in the year. I play the video for her I looked at my phone just in time to see Marcus smashing her face in her birthday cake. Justice turned to him and gave him a big kiss putting cake on his face as we all laughed. Everyone was so happy; we didn't have not one care in the world. Justice smiled at the phone. I sat her on the couch to watch the videos and look at pictures of Marcus, and I walked away. This shit was eating me alive. The pain cut so deep that I just knew I would never get over it.

"You're ready to go, babe?" Takhiya walked up behind me asking as she touched my shoulder. I was burning up on the inside because I really didn't want her to touch me right now. The only thing I wanted no one in the world could give me. I knew I had to get over it and quick before I did something I would regret. I gritted my teeth a little.

"Yeah ma, let's get this over with." I took deep breaths to calm down, then grabbed her hand. She waddled beside me as I went to the living room to get Justice. I helped them with their coats and walked out the house to the limo that was waiting on us.

We were the last ones to pull up to the funeral. Once we arrived, Pierre and Marcell stepped out of the limousines they were in. We all were dressed in black Gucci suits with a royal blue tie. I helped Takhiya and Justice out of the car as Marcell helped Bailey out. Our women had on royal blue match matching our ties. Bailey had on a pants suit, and Takhiya had on a dress that fitted her pregnant body nicely. Justice stepped out of the limo in her gray and baby blue Jordan's that Marcus had gotten her the day he was killed, and a gray matching jogging suit.

Natalie walked out of the church to meet us.

"Sorry for you guys loss. You know that I loved Marcus. I love you all to, but when the funeral is over, we need to talk." I nodded my head at Natalie, and we all walked into church together.

I sat on the front row in a daze. I had to find a way to get over the resentment that I was feeling. I looked at the casket as some lady was singing, and all I could think was that Marcus wouldn't want me to feel like this towards my wife. He had grown to love Takhiya like a sister. As if she knew what I was thinking, Takhiya squeezed my hand as she wiped a tear that had escaped from her eye. I looked around at my brothers. Pierre was sitting there like he was in shock and Marcell was trying his hardest to keep it together. I heard whimpering, and I looked at Justice who was crying her little heart out and held my baby trying to smooth the pain that we all were holding inside.

❧ 28 ❧

PIERRE

I hate funerals and what I hate more than funerals were graveyards. This was always the hardest part for me putting my people in the ground. That was so final. Once you went in, there everyone knows there was no way of coming back out. I was in my own personal hell; this was the second time I didn't protect my brothers. I was busy worried about this operation and money that it led us to lose our brother. I could've done that job on my own, but I just had to ask Marcell and Bryce to handle it with me. Truth is I was being selfish. My brothers were so caught up in these two bitches' pussies that I barely had time with them.

Not only that, motherfuckas in Miami was starting to think we were soft and that they could move in on us because we weren't present. Guilt was eating at me, and there was no way I would ever get over this. I'm the oldest, and my job is to protect each one of my brothers even if it cost me my life. When we were younger, I kept Marcus close to me. It's true that Marcell and Marcus had that Irish twin connection. They knew what each other was thinking and damn near felt what each other was feeling, but Marcus was my heart. When he was born, I would keep him under me.

I would do the shit that big brothers did when they had siblings like get them in trouble for getting on my nerves. Marcus was my man; through all the dirt that I couldn't do, I had him to do it. He was my sidekick— everyone needed one.

Look, you know Olivia dad's been on my ass about fucking that hoe he calls a daughter. Every time we're in a room together he gets disrespectful and just wants me to sit there and take that shit."

Marcus hit the blunt I had rolled and just nodded his head as he exhaled the smoke. Marcus was fifteen at the time, but I let him do whatever he wanted to do with me. Hell, we were brothers, and if he didn't do it with us, he was going to do it with his friends. I didn't trust any of them. We were all born into money and stayed in a predominantly white community, so most of his friends where buying coke and meth from us. They basically said fuck weed, but I wasn't going to have that shit with my brother.

"Dad has his own agenda with the old man. I need to teach him a lesson, and you know I can't get close to him after I backhanded his old ass like the bitch he is." Marcus laughed.

"Yeah, that was fucked up bro, for real. You had his old ass looking like one of those I'm falling and can't get up commercials. Papi was so pissed off." I laughed at him.

"The only thing he loves just as much as his daughters are those ugly ass Doberman Pinschers I need you to take care of that shit for me, bro."

"I got you, bro, don't worry."

About two days passed before the old man called my dad yelling through the phone. I turned and looked at Marcus who had a smirk on his face, and he turned and walked out of my dad's study. A couple of days later, I found out that Marcus had given the dog some bakers chocolate with rat poison and antifreeze in it. That lil' nigga wanted to make sure the job was done.

I laughed thinking about all the shit I got him into and got him out of, but death was one thing he couldn't come back from.

We walked into Bryce's house, and I still wasn't in the mood to be bothered, but whatever Natalie had to say I was ready to listen. Plus, I had some shit that I needed to get off my chest. My brothers were going to pissed, but fuck it, ain't no holding back now. As soon as Natalie got there, we all went to the basement.

"Bryce and Marcell, I don't know what's going on with y'all and these girls, but you all have to fix it."

"What do you mean us and these girl? Takhiya is my wife and having my seed; there's no girls around here."

"And I plan on marrying Bailey as soon as I can; life is too short not to be happy."

I was fed up with this shit. Whatever Natalie had to say could wait, I had to speak my mind.

"Look, when we first found out Bailey and Takhiya were coming to Miami, we were supposed to use that bitch to get that nigga LaQuan for taking our shit. No one told you two dummies to fall the fuck in love and marry this bitch. LaQuan and both of them were supposed to be dead by now, not one fucking having my niece or nephew and the other one is going to be my sister-in-law. Both of you niggas are fuck boys and that's the reason Marcus is in a fucking grave now." Natalie looked at all of us.

"I don't care what's going on you need to handle this shit with LaQuan. I'm getting calls from Italy over his death. You niggas are playing in my backyard now, and I have to cover y'all ass on every end. Kill this nigga and get it over with. There's no reason that all of us are after the same person, and he's like fucking Casper because we can't find his ass. Do what you need to do and kill whoever you need to get this job done." Natalie walked away from us.

"Pierre, don't fucking touch those girls. They haven't done shit but been a pawn in the game you all have played, but couldn't carry out correct. You can't help who love, but you can help who you kill." Natalie left us down there to think about what she said.

"What's the new plan?" Marcell asked, looking at Bryce.

🦋 29 🦋

TAKHIYA

I stood at the basement door shocked, listening to what Pierre was saying. We were just a part of a fucking plot. I couldn't believe this shit I have damn near lost my life twice fucking with this man. All that I love you shit meant nothing to him I guess. Then to find out that he wanted to kill me just fucked me up even more. Natalie was on her way up the stairs, so I walked in the kitchen acting like I was getting a glass of water. I walked into the room I was sharing with my lying ass husband and packed a small bag.

I was tired of niggas walking all over me and treating me like I wasn't shit. I went to the safe in the wall and took all the money that was in there. I was never coming back to this motherfucka, and I needed money to raise my son. I picked up a picture of Justice off the dresser and tucked it in the bag I had. I felt like my world was shattering around me, and I didn't have a way out. I walked out of the room to peeking through the hallway to make sure they hadn't come upstairs. I walked to the front door looked around then grabbed the keys to my truck off the key holder on the wall.

Tears rolled down my face as I thought about the fact that my own husband was setting me up.

"Call Bailey." My car repeated my command before dialing Bailey's number.

"Yeah, Khiya."

"You need to pack some clothes and leave. These niggas that are pretending to be the love of our lives want to kill us." I hung up the phone and drove down one of my old blocks.

I was broken, and I knew the only thing that would make this pain go away was what I was staying away from all these years. I pulled up to one of my old dealer's sons. When he saw me, he had a big smile on his face. I knew that he would remember me because I took his virginity when I was like twelve.

"What are doing around these parts?"

"Cain, I need some coke."

"Are giving special favors for this because I remember how you used to get down."

When that came out of his mouth, it made my skin crawl to think of letting these niggas putting their hands on me. I looked in the bag that I had stuffed with money and pulled out a stack on hundreds.

"These are not the old days; I pay for my shit." I slapped the money into his hands and waited for him to come back with my merchandise.

I pulled into the garage and closed it back, I know that this would probably be the first place Bryce would look for me, but I didn't give a fuck. He planned to kill me so I might as well take my fate by doing something that I loved. I went into my office and turned on the desk light. I took the letter opener and cut through the brick of coke I had just purchased. The white powder was on the table in a pile.

I sat there thinking of all the shit I've been through throughout my life. I have only had two real relationships, and both of those niggas crossed me. I felt like God was turning his back on me, once again. I have never had an easy life. I've just always tried to make the best of it. There were only two times in life that I felt like killing myself, and today is one of those days. I don't know whether it's my fault for fucking with grimy ass niggas, or the niggas fault for fucking over me. I was a lost soul, and I had no one in the world to save me. I have been up then down for so long that this shit doesn't even matter anymore.

I cut me some lines of powder from the pile and thought about the movie *Scarface* when Tony Montana sat at the desk with a huge pile of cocaine in front of him.

"Say hello to my little friend," I quoted the famous line before laughing.

My phone started ringing off the hook. It was no one but Bryce so I put his ass on do not disturb and continued to think about what my life could be like if I hadn't met two fuck niggas. I thought about Bryce with this mob shit. I guess that life isn't for me since he wants to take my ass out anyway. I felt like the life I lived was an entire urban fiction romance novel that went wrong. Where the fuck is that nigga that makes me fall for him and does me right at the end of this bitch? Now I just get the nigga on the down low, the nigga that damn near kills me, and the mob nigga that will succeed.

My life has really been fucked up since birth. I sat there just looking at the best thing that has ever happened to me. The only thing that would make all the hurt and pain go away, the only thing that will numb me and make me forget the pain. I rubbed my stomach knowing I would never get a chance to hold my baby. He was moving like crazy.

"Hey, little one! Mommy may never get the chance to know you but know I love with every beat of my heart. My entire life has been fucked up, and I know the only thing I would do is fuck up yours even worst. Be a good boy for mommy and know I will be watching over you from heaven.

BOOM!!!

TO BE CONTINUED...

CPSIA information can be obtained
at www.ICGtesting.com
Printed in the USA
LVHW04s2301180518
577693LV00011B/746/P